The Man of My Dreams

By

Gladys Quintal

The Man of my Dreams
By Gladys Quintal
Editing by M. R. Saxton
Copyright 2011 Gladys Quintal

ISBN-10: 1466415088

ISBN-13: 978-1466415089

Dedication

*The Man of my Dream*s is inspired by my favourite
TV show of all time, *Moonlight.*

To my own dark haired man, Barry, who I dreamed of
long before I met him.

To my beautiful children who make life worth living.

To my wonderful friends Hayley and Moyra for
egging me on and being my #1 fans.

To Nana for giving me that kick in the butt I needed
and helping to get my creative juices flowing again.

To Tracy for making me believe I could do anything I
put my mind to.

And to my Aunty Sherrie who always has my back.

I love you all. xx

Prologue

Usually secluded this time of night, the streets of Perth had an unusual volume of the homeless. He'd been forced to feed on them once or twice—hunger ruled, although he much preferred his favourite food source. Always remorseful afterwards, he hated the being he'd become. Evil, it was the evil he loved most to snuff out. The blood of evil men gave him strength and satisfied his hunger more than any other. There was certainly no shortage of evil in this city. The trouble was finding it in time, before it had the chance to kill or take the virtue of an innocent. It was those times he had a sense of pride and felt almost like a hero . . . instead of the sickening, vile monster he really was.

He could still remember being human. He missed it more than he ever thought possible. He missed mortality and the prospect of growing old— qualities he no longer possessed. He knew many humans who longed to be like him. Fools! They couldn't possibly understand what his existence was really like. Hunting others and being so desperate for blood that almost any meal would do. Once the bloodlust took over he was powerless, resulting in the haunting regrets he was now trying to right. He missed the love of a woman terribly, a human woman. And really, what woman in her right mind could love a creature such as him? She would shy away in terror if she saw him in his real form. He cringed inwardly, knowing her reaction to his hunger and hunting lusts would break his heart.

Or what was left of his heart.

Sure, there were fantasy stories of how his kind could survive on stored blood. But in reality, only blood that came from a warm mammal with a beating heart would suffice. Anything else would just make him weak and anaemic. He needed his strength now more than ever. His mission, after all, was ridding the streets of evil.

He'd been roaming these same streets now for more than 20 years. It only seemed logical that at some point the evil would be purged. But as soon as he got rid of one monstrous human another was not far behind. So he wandered and listened intently for the cries of another innocent victim. This stupid curse only allowed him to be seen in human form through a mortal's subconscious. This made things even more complicated. When victims were fully awake and alert, they saw him as he truly was. This petrified them more than the human monsters he was rescuing them from. Surely tonight, just like any other night, someone would need him. He listened and waited, hoping it would not be too long. He was getting very hungry.

Chapter 1
End of a Nightmare

Cassandra cowered under her covers. She could hear her mother and stepfather arguing. They'd been drinking again as they did every payday. She hated to hear the way they yelled obscenities at each other and the screams of her mother when it got beyond arguing. Her stepfather would take out his frustrations, blaming her because he was worthless and a hopeless husband and father. He had never really been a man, but rather a fat ugly slob who thought the world revolved around him. In his mind, everyone should bow to him.

Only God knew why he had such a high opinion of himself. Everyone hated him and her mother was far too pretty to be married to an ogre. She, too, had become a pathetic excuse for a parent these days. She could hardly protect herself, let alone her 13-year-old daughter. She worked full time at the local hospital laundry, a thankless job, always stinking hot. Then she would be expected to come home and prepare meals for him as well as keeping a spotless house. When he got home from work he'd go and have a shower, then sit on the couch for the rest of the night expecting her to wait on him. Cassandra, too, would be made to help around the house. Doing the laundry, washing dishes, and helping with meals were her lot in life while the lazy slob sat on his fat arse, belly hanging over his jeans, drinking beer and watching TV.

She hated him with a vengeance, praying every night that he would not make it home from work, fantasizing about car accidents or heart attacks. . . anything sparing her from ever seeing his ugly face again. She knew in her heart that her mother would never leave him. Traumatized by the divorce and struggling as a single parent, she settled for this loser. He was the ugliest man Cassandra had ever seen in her life and still could not believe her mother had seen anything in him to begin with. With his skinny white legs and big fat stomach he reminded her of a frog, and a slimy one at that.

He was always putting her mum down, calling her fat and ugly. He should look in the mirror! Her mother had started going to meetings every Tuesday night to try and lose weight for him. And that is when the visits to Cassie's bedroom had started. At first he had just tried kissing and fondling her, totally grossing her out. She told her mother after the first time. Yet her mother just dismissed it and told her he was just trying to show his affection . . . and not to be a little slut and encourage him. Her words had cut deep and now Cassie kept her thoughts to herself, no longer trusting her mother to save her from this monster.

After a while the fondling was not enough and one night he came into her room with her mother's lubricant and raped her. Afterwards he laughed at her and told her that if she ever told her mother he would tell her that she had seduced him. "Of course your mother will believe me over you, her whore of a daughter," he said as he left the room, leaving her feeling dirty and sore. What had she ever done to deserve parents like these? She held on to the hope that her life would be good if only she could get through the next few years.

God, how she wished she had a Guardian Angel to take her away from all this!

Eventually things got even worse. She could hear furniture breaking and what she assumed was her mother being thrown around the room. Her mother screamed and was shouting something that Cassie couldn't decipher.

The front door slammed and then all went quiet. Cassie's heart was beating so loud that she could hear it in her ears. *One night he is going to kill my mum,* she thought. Her bedroom door slowly started to open.

Please be mum, please be mum, Cassie pleaded silently. But she knew in her heart that it wasn't.

He almost fell onto her bed, staggering and swearing.

"Your fucking bitch of a mother has walked out on us. Fuck her, we don't need her anyway!"

Cassie's head was spinning. How could her mum walk out and leave her alone with this monster. What kind of a mother was she? The ogre started to unbutton his pants.

"You're a good girl, you know what daddy wants."

She felt sick and decided he wasn't going to rape her anymore. She would fight him with all she had and die trying if need be. What kind of a life was it anyway? She'd be better off dead.

He took off his pants and started to climb onto her bed. She kicked at him and he almost fell over. He wasn't at all happy and punched her really hard in the head. She screamed and bit and scratched, making him very angry. He grabbed her around the throat and choked her. She could feel her life draining away. He was calling her names and swearing and squeezing. He smelled of stale beer and cigarettes. His face was so close to hers that she could see all the veins sticking out in his forehead. She tried to fight but he was too strong.

Please someone help me, she pleaded silently.

And there He was.

The Guardian Angel she had prayed for was there. At least he certainly looked like an angel, tall with dark hair and the most beautiful eyes she had ever seen. He was standing behind her stepfather smiling at her. Maybe he had come to take her to the other side? She felt calm and stopped fighting. The darkness came and she slipped away.

Her mother came home an hour later. She found Cassie unconscious in her bed and her husband was nowhere to be found. She tried to wake Cassie, who was incoherent and rambling about an angel. The poor girl couldn't be brought around. Frantic, Cassie's mother rang an ambulance wondering in the back of her mind where her husband was and if he'd done this to her daughter.

She had to get away from him. She had to be safe, not just for her own sake but for her daughter's as well. She made the decision on the way to the hospital that he'd never hurt either of them again.

She rang the police and told them her husband had tried to strangle her daughter. They were dispatched to the hospital and put out an APB. It didn't take long to find him. His car was down by the beach. Inside were the remains of his body, ripped to pieces like it had been attacked by some sort of animal. Strangely, the doors were all locked and the windows rolled up. There was no evidence of anyone else ever being inside the car.

Dental records confirmed it was definitely him and forensics found nothing to explain what had killed him. It had been the third crime like this in as many weeks. It seemed the police had a serial killer on their hands with no clues on who he was or a motive for the killings. The only similarity in the three cases involved ramblings from each victim about a dark haired angel. All gave the same description of this tall, dark and handsome man who appeared out of nowhere just as they thought they were dying. This Guardian Angel saved them from their assailants and left behind no footprints, fingerprints or DNA of any kind. He, somehow, gained access to residences when all the doors and windows were locked. Obviously these were going to be extremely challenging cases to solve!

Chapter 2
De Ja Vu

Cassie slipped in and out of consciousness, rambling about the man who had saved her. It seemed she was reliving the nightmare over and over again, crying out at times. Doctors concluded the man was a figment of her imagination, invented by her to save her from the abuse she'd suffered from her stepfather. They found extensive faded bruising and evidence of continual sexual abuse. Her mother had cried, ashamed. She hadn't listened to her daughter's pleas about her husband's advances. She thought Cassie was exaggerating his motives. Cassie hadn't told her how far it had gone. No wonder . . . It's not like she'd been much of a mother to the poor girl over the last few years. Why? Why had she let that bully of a man drag her down so low?

She sat at Cassie's bedside praying her daughter would recover without serious brain damage. The poor child had suffered an oxygen shortage while that bastard's hands had been around her throat. She'd never forgive herself if her baby died or never totally regained consciousness.

She was consoled by Cassie's father, who sat beside her and held her hand. She rang him when they got to the hospital. They hadn't spoken in the last two years and he hadn't seen Cassie— not because he hadn't wanted to, but because it was too painful to see the love of his life with such a man. He had tried to get his ex-wife and daughter to come away with him, but that man had some sort of hold over them and his ex-wife's spirit seemed broken.

He should never have let it happen in the first place. His stupid midlife crisis had caused him to let her down. He'd succumbed to the flattery of a younger attractive female workmate. Harmless flirting turned into a liaison at a seedy motel. He regretted it as soon as it happened. God, how he loved his wife! What was wrong with him? Of course she saw the signs and left him. He begged for forgiveness, but he'd shattered her trust and she felt humiliated and worthless. She took Cassie and they left. He hadn't tried hard enough to get them back.

This is my fault, he thought to himself and he started to sob.

His ex-wife turned to him and squeezed his hand tighter. She still loved him and knew he was blaming himself, just as she was. Her heart went out to him.

Cassie stirred.

"Mum," she muttered. "Where am I? My throat hurts."

Her mother burst into tears. She jumped up and grabbed her daughter's hand.

"I'm here baby. It's okay. You're safe now."

"Where's dad, and has he finished painting my room yet?"

Her parents looked at one another not sure what to say. Her father had been painting her room the day before her mother left. She had picked a bright pink colour for the walls and a pretty green for drapes and bedding. He finished painting the room and it hadn't been touched since the day they separated. Her father stood up.

"Yes, Sweetie, I finished it and it looks beautiful."

"Cool, Daddy! When can we go home?"

He squeezed his wife's hand and looked into her eyes.

"When the doctor says you can, Hun," he assured her.

They were both crying now.

"What happened to me?" Cassie asked.

"We're not sure, Baby . . . Do you remember anything?"

Cassie frowned and tried to think. All she could remember was being excited because her father had brought the paint home and was prepping her room ready to start painting. Her mother sighed and hoped that Cassie's memory loss would be permanent, sparing her from the horrors of what her so-called husband had put the innocent girl through this last year.

"Don't worry about it too much, Sweetie. You need to rest now so you can heal faster."

Cassie had to admit she was tired and let her heavy eyelids close.

The doctor came in and her father pulled him aside.

"She doesn't remember anything about the attack. She doesn't remember the last two years at all!"

The doctor assured him it was normal with this type of trauma— it was the mind's way of dealing with such things. Her memory might return gradually or never at all. It was hard to tell with these cases. Her father, like her mother, prayed it never would.

Outside in the corridor Cassie's parents made a pact. They would try and put their marriage back together and let Cassie forget that the last two years ever happened. Certainly she'd realise things had changed and that she'd grown older . . . but she'd never have to know about her father's affair or the horrible man who had taken her innocence and almost her life. They would think of a way to explain the attack and tell her the man had been found dead. Cassie would never need to worry about him trying again. Together they would put their shattered lives back together for the sake of their daughter and never speak of it again. They would be a family as they should have always been.

Chapter 3
Shattered Dreams

It had been a long night. We always seemed to be short staffed at the hospital these days and literally run off our feet. At last, I was home. All I could think of was jumping in the shower and snuggling up to Paul, who was sound asleep. It was 2 a.m., after all. A two whole week's holiday stretched before me. I couldn't wait for the morning.

I let the hot water run over my body for 20 minutes. It felt so good, relaxing my aching muscles. I dried myself and walked into the bedroom naked, the cool air feeling good on my skin. I slid in between the sheets and snuggled up behind Paul, looking forward to a sound sleep. Startled, Paul pulled away from me and moved to the other side of the bed. I was taken aback.

"What's wrong?" I asked.

"Nothing," he replied groggily. "I'm just tired."

I was beyond hurt. He'd never done that before. It wasn't like I was trying to seduce him. I just wanted to cuddle him and go to sleep. Now I felt sad and alone, wondering what was going on in his head. So much for a peaceful night's rest, I'd be worrying all night.

It took me ages to finally sleep. I tossed and turned, trying not to cry. It occurred to me how dependent I'd become, needing Paul's warm back to lull me into dreamland. But eventually exhaustion worked its magic.

The same reoccurring dream filled my subconscious. The dark haired man, once again, joined me in the sleep realm. I have no idea who he is or where he came from, but I've been dreaming about him for years. He'd been present in my dreams since I was 17 and lost my parents in that horrible car crash.

We'd been out together for dinner and a movie and were on our way home. Out of nowhere a drunk driver veered across the centre line and hit us head on. I was the only survivor and mysteriously ended up at the hospital just moments after the accident happened. No one could explain it, except that maybe some Good Samaritan driving past had dropped me off and left before the police could ask questions. I couldn't remember anything about the accident or how I had possibly survived. I certainly had no knowledge of the person who rescued me. It was a tough time in my life, being alone and orphaned at such a young age, hospitalized for weeks.

Perhaps this tragedy drew me to nursing. After I was discharged, I decided to enroll in nursing training and have worked in the profession ever since. I met Paul, a friend of a friend, 10 years later. We seemed to click straight away and within a few months had moved in together.

My dreams about the dark haired man are always happy. I have no idea if he is real, a figment of my imagination, or someone I knew in a past life. He always makes me feel safe and protected in his arms. I never felt completely alone even during the loneliest times of my life. Maybe I invented him to help cope with the huge loss of my parents? I really don't know where he came from but am very glad he lives somewhere in my dreams.

He visited me again tonight.

I'd been restless, drifting in and out of reality before hearing his voice.

Are you okay, Cassandra? Whispered my dark haired man.

I'm so confused! I confided. *I don't understand why Paul is being so cold to me. Everything seemed fine until I got home from work tonight. Now he's acting strange and I have no idea what's going on!*

My dark haired man took me in his arms and pulled me close to him, so safe and warm. It felt like home.

I am so lucky to have you, I said, looking up into those soft green eyes. He always made me feel so wonderful, like nothing could ever hurt me. *What did I ever do to deserve you?*

He pulled away and led me to the grass, emerald green in the sunlight. I stood over him as he sat, relaxed. It was such a beautiful day, as it always was in my dreams. Soft grass, wildflowers everywhere, birds were singing . . . and of course his presence. I could feel the sunlight on my face and the scent of lavender filled the air. I felt so loved when I was with him, so at peace.

Why can't I feel like this all the time? I thought to myself. Of course, he heard my thoughts.

I'm the lucky one, he said, smiling up at me. I thought I saw a flicker of sadness in his eyes. *You have given me so much, more than you will ever know, Cassandra.*

I sat down next to him and took his hand in mine. He smiled that beautiful smile, melting my heart and then leaned towards me. My cheek warmed from his soft kiss. His chest and arms enveloped me, pulling me around my waist . . . against him.

I'll be here as long as you need me.

I woke in the morning to find Paul had already left for work. He hadn't even come in to kiss me goodbye. Something was definitely wrong. I dragged myself out of bed and slipped on my dressing gown, stomach churning. I hadn't a clue what had happened. The day before everything seemed fine. What had suddenly changed so drastically? Why was Paul so cold to me? I picked up the phone and tried ringing his mobile. It went straight to voice mail. I left a message for him to ring me back and then made myself a cup of tea. I sat down on the couch, worried.

A million things ran through my head. Was it something I'd said or done? I couldn't think of anything. We visited his mum and dad for lunch yesterday and everything seemed fine. His sister had cut my hair and he'd been really attentive. He even told me I looked beautiful. What possibly could have changed between then and my shift at the hospital?

What had I done?

The phone rang and I almost jumped out of my skin. It was Paul. He said he had a lot on his mind and not to worry too much. His workmate had died a couple of months ago and he had been under a lot of stress at work.

"It isn't you," he assured me. "You haven't done anything and we'll talk properly when I get home."

I felt relieved. Perhaps it really was just work stress. Feeling better, I set about getting dressed and planning what to do with the wonderful two weeks I had off.

I was chatting on the phone to a friend of mine, Maria, when Paul turned up. He'd come home for lunch. I said goodbye to Maria and hung up the phone, happy to see him. As I approached him with a hug, he dodged me. "We need to talk, Cassandra," he announced. Uh oh, there went that churning in my stomach again. He kept his distance. It made me feel really uneasy.

"Okay, Paul. What is going on?" I asked.

"I've been doing a lot of thinking," he said, somber and reserved. "I'm just not sure if I still want to get married and have kids anytime soon."

I was shocked.

Where was this coming from? We'd been planning to get married and have a baby for years. Why this sudden about turn?

"Alright," I responded shakily, trying to stay calm. "We can wait a while longer." *But how much longer?* I was 33 and felt my biological clock ticking. We'd been together for nearly six years and the whole time he knew I always wanted kids. At this moment I felt a bit cheated. Cheated and torn. I loved him and didn't want to lose him.

"We can wait until you are sure," I continued, dreading his response.

"I don't know if I'll ever be ready. Hell, I'm not sure I even want kids. I know you do, though, and that you're getting to the age that it might be getting harder to conceive. I don't want to stop you from having a family . . . so I think we should break up, Cassandra."

He was dead serious.

"Break up?" I cried. "Yes, Paul, I do want kids but I don't want to lose you! Can't we talk about this? I'm sure I'll be fine if I don't end up being a mum. Can't we compromise somehow?"

"No," he said sternly. "The honest truth is, I don't think I even love you anymore. I don't want to spend the rest of my life with you."

It was a knife in my heart. The shock nearly floored me. I was crying now, an uncontrollable reaction to this unthinkable statement. What had just happened? Had he just dumped me? This was like a nightmare! If it had been building up and I could see the tell-tale signs, maybe it wouldn't have come as such a blow. But I honestly could not think of a single reason, not one little hint, that foreshadowed Paul's words.

He watched my reaction, unmoved.

"I'll come home tonight after work and pick up some stuff. I'm going to stay with mum and dad for a while."

"You're moving out? Don't you want to talk about this some more?"

"No, I've made up mind. I'm sorry, but I can't help the way I feel." With that he turned around and left me a crying heap on the couch.

I felt as if I had been punched in the stomach. It was all so sudden. I was miserable and mourned on the couch for the rest of the day. The wait was unbearable as I braced myself for him to come home and get his things.

He turned up around 5 p.m. When he saw the state I was in he came over and gave me a hug.

"I'm so sorry, Cassandra. I don't know what came over me. Of course I'm not going to leave you."

I was reeling from the roller coaster of emotions. Relief flooded me. I rationalized that poor Paul had simply been in a bad state of mind. He saw the error of his ways and knew this was where he wanted to be. Everything was going to work out, right? I comforted myself with these thoughts.

He had to go out for a few hours for work but would be back that evening. We'd sort everything out properly then. He kissed me and departed, leaving my head spinning. For the next several hours I pondered the situation. Paul was like a yoyo, wavering back and forth, leaving then not leaving. I clung to his assurance but, honestly, was unsettled. To clear my head I ran a warm bath and soaked in it for ages. I climbed into bed, exhausted.

He turned up around 11 p.m. and started packing up his stuff. He left that night. I never really found out what had happened but a year later he was married. Not long after that his first child was born. I guess it wasn't that he wasn't ready. He just didn't want to do any of it with me.

Paul's abrupt departure turned my whole world upside down. I couldn't eat. I couldn't sleep. My stomach hurt all the time and I couldn't stop crying. After a few days of suffering I went to the doctor to get something to help me to sleep. That, plus a few glasses of wine, seemed to do the trick . . . until I woke every new morning faced with reality. Thank God for timing. I didn't have to report to work and had the remainder of my time off to pull myself together.

I tried to start planning my future. *Let's see, what should I do from here?* I couldn't think straight. Everything had changed. I had no family and didn't want to burden my friends. Once again I decided to take a sleeping pill, go to bed, and deal with it later. I felt the drug working and slowly started to drift off to sleep.

A warm body cuddled up behind me. I tried to open my eyes but they were too heavy from the sedative. I could feel kisses on the back of my neck. A hand caressed my stomach. Soft fingers touched my breasts, slowly moving down my body. I pushed myself backwards and snuggled into them, so relaxing, so arousing. I let the sensations take over, drifting in and out of sleep, seeming to dream . . . but it felt so real, very real.

Someone was on top of me. My arms were wrapped around his waist and my legs rested over his. I could feel the soft strokes inside me gently bringing me to orgasm. The sensation was so intense that I managed to open my eyes . . . but could see no one. My arms were still wrapped around my invisible lover and I was quivering slightly. It was so familiar and I felt no fear.

I'm in a drug induced dream, I thought to myself and fell back into a deep sleep.

I woke with a start at 3 a.m. feeling groggy from the sleeping pill. I thought I heard something outside and decided to go out onto the balcony to take a look. My legs were heavy and my eyes didn't want to open properly. I opened the sliding door and walked out into the night, relishing the cool air. It felt wonderful against my skin, sensitive and still a little aroused from the dream. I looked around but couldn't figure out where the noise was coming from or even what the noise was. Curious, I looked out over the railing, leaning further than was safe in my impaired state. Something moved out of the corner of my eye, startling me. I lost my balance and the next thing I knew . . . I was falling. It was surreal. I wasn't frightened and remember thinking that perhaps the pain in my heart would soon be over. I wasn't afraid of dying; it might be the easiest way out of all this.

I felt strong arms around me and warm breath on my neck. Then everything faded to black.

Chapter 4
Dream Lover

I woke in the morning feeling like I'd just had the most wonderful night's sleep in my life. I vaguely remembered falling from the balcony and someone catching me. I must have been dreaming about Him again. Oddly, I felt renewed— calm and in control for the first time in days. My stomach no longer churned and my head felt clear again. Today was the first day of the rest of my life and I was going to start living it!

I got up, showered and decided to get dressed in something nice and summery. I found a pretty dress and decided to venture out. I wanted breakfast in the sunshine. I felt alive again, better than I had in years. I didn't know what had bought on this sudden change in mood . . . but I liked it!

I was sitting at the table outside Dome Cafe drinking coffee, eating pancakes, and reading the paper. I felt a hand on my shoulder. I spun around but there was no one there. Was it just my imagination? As I went back to the paper a wonderful, warm sensation spread up my body. Euphoria, almost drug-like, caused me to catch my breath. Wow, what a feeling! My whole body felt alive and almost glowing. If pancakes in the sun could do this, I would eat here every morning! I no longer missed Paul and the anguish of him leaving had all but disappeared. Instead, I had a sense of wellbeing and utter happiness. I didn't feel the slightest bit lonely and was looking forward to the rest of the day.

What to do now, maybe a bit of shopping? I could do with some new shoes. A woman could always do with new shoes! I still had 10 days of my holiday left. I owned a beach house in Lancelin left to me by my parents. The weather was beautiful. The shops were beckoning. I decided I should grab some new clothes and a new bathing suit while I was at it. Then I'd go to the beach for a few days. Excited, I couldn't wait to start my holiday!

Although my parent's death left a void that would never quite be filled, I was fortunate they'd left me quite well set up. I didn't want for much as the interest on their estate was enough to live on comfortably. The family house in Ellenbrook was freehold. I didn't really have to work but enjoyed my job and needed to do something to keep busy.

I withdrew a few grand from my account and went on a shopping spree. Morley Galleria, here I come! Morley was only about 20 minutes from Ellenbrook and had an excellent mall. Going all out I bought new dresses, bathing suits, shoes and perfume. I loaded it all into my jeep and headed off to the beach. I would grab a few supplies in the little shopping centre there . . . I could already taste the wine and chocolate!

The day was gorgeous and I felt invigorated. I turned the radio up loud and sang along. It was a miracle to feel so wonderful after just a few short days of being dumped. I honestly had never felt better. The beach was only an hour's drive from Morley and it was still quite early in the day when I arrived.

The house looked cosy and inviting, just as I remembered it. I couldn't wait to unpack the jeep and haul my stuff inside. It was a little musty as all the curtains were drawn. I hadn't used it in a while. I opened up all the windows, turned on the stereo and started putting away my new clothes. On went the bathing suit, as there was still plenty of time for a swim. It was very flattering and showed my figure off well. Not that I needed any confidence at the moment . . . I was flying high! I grabbed a towel and dashed down to the water.

The beach was deserted. It was spring and not a lot of the people from Perth would think it was warm enough to go swimming. There were a few people at the pub just down the beach, but my little spot in paradise was still quite secluded— just the way I like it!

The water, a little cold at first, made me gasp. But I soon acclimated and enjoyed the coolness of the waves moving over me. The water here was so clean and clear. All my senses were alive and even the water touching my skin felt amazing. I went up on to the sand and grabbed my towel. As I dried myself I felt a kiss on my check and then hot breath on my neck. I spun around. This time I saw a wisp of what looked like smoke but again no one was there. I was sure I hadn't imagined it this time . . . could my mind be playing tricks on me? It hadn't changed my mood but left me a little intrigued..

I went back up to the house and had a quick shower. I jumped back into the jeep and headed to the shop to grab some wine, chocs and a TV dinner. I thought about going down to the pub for dinner, but I'd been there a few times with Paul. I felt like a bit of a loser going on my own, so down to the little shopping centre I went. The shop had a good selection of DVD's. I grabbed a couple of my favourite flicks and headed back.

With dinner in the microwave and a bottle of wine opened, I put on a DVD and snuggled down on the couch. It felt so comfortable sitting there, eating my dinner and drinking wine.

Wow, this is the life, I sighed, quite drowsy and content.

He was back and utterly gorgeous. Dark hair and green eyes, tall and muscular, and that smile . . . it took my breath away. And he's all mine! He was lying on the couch shirtless with his arm around me. I had my head on his shoulder. He stroked my hair, telling me how much he loved me. I felt so happy and content. Life was wonderful. He lifted my face to his.

I love you and you can be sure that I will always be here for you no matter what. I'll never leave you as he did.

I knew he meant it. His eyes were so sincere and I felt overwhelmed and completely loved for the first time in my life. He kissed me tenderly at first. His lips were soft and moist. I felt a surge of warmth flooding my body. Then his kisses became more urgent and I felt like I would utterly explode with desire. I wanted him to make love to me desperately.

He started to unbutton my blouse and then slipped it over my shoulders, all the while kissing me passionately. He rolled towards me and pressed himself against me. I could feel him hot and hard and hear his breathing getting heavier. I'd never felt so out of control in my life! He undid my bra and gently started caressing my breasts. Every part of my body was alive and aching for him now. I couldn't hold back any longer and started to rub up against him while unbuttoning his shorts. Oh, how I wanted to rip his pants off! Within minutes he was above me and then inside me. Oh my God, it felt good! He was so hard and I could feel every inch. I lost myself in the moment and relaxed completely. This was so amazing and I didn't want it to end. Every part of my body felt unbelievable. My skin was awakened to every sensation, every touch. He kissed my neck, my lips, my breasts….

Please don't be over quickly. I wanted this feeling to last forever.

I shouldn't have worried. He took me to the edge and then stopped, leaving me begging for more time and time again. He teased me over and over then rewarded me by making my whole body shake with ecstasy. Every stroke felt like heaven. His body was so beautiful and felt so at home between my legs. His lovemaking took me to the heights of ecstasy as I felt myself shuddering against him again and again— my first ever multiple orgasm!

I was totally exhausted but felt wonderful. I had never been made love to like that and never felt such rapture, such love. I was totally and utterly satisfied. He was the most amazing and considerate lover. I snuggled up to him and he smiled at me and pulled me close.

Always remember that I love you, no matter what. Promise me.

I promise, I replied. *I love you too.*

We lay there for ages with him stroking my hair.

I woke to the sun streaming through the window. I was lying alone on the couch and was fully dressed! I felt a little confused. Had it been a dream? Surely I couldn't dream that! I got up and started to search the house for my dream lover. There was no sign of anyone else ever being there. I must have fallen asleep watching DVD's and dreamt the whole thing. I sat down, puzzled. It certainly felt real, very real. And my body still remembered his touch vividly. What was going on? Was I losing it?

I was puzzled. Where did he come from? Obviously, he wasn't here last night before I fell asleep on the couch. I didn't even know his name. But he must be the dark haired man that I dreamt of almost every night. Was my dream lover actually visiting me or was this just a figment of my imagination? I felt disappointed but at the same time strangely content. Once again I had that amazing feeling as if I was finally alive and nothing could ever hurt me again. If it was just a dream . . . well, then I would look forward to going to sleep every night!

Chapter 5
Daydreaming

As my holiday at the beach house flew by, I enjoyed the beautiful weather, lovely beach, awesome views, peace, tranquility . . . and wonderful dreams!

I resigned myself to the fact that I'd dreamt the whole experience with my lover. Maybe, somehow, it was more than that . . . but all I knew was that every time I was totally relaxed or asleep he was there. I slept late, swam in the ocean, read, watched movies and just totally regenerated from the devastation I felt just over a week ago. And in my dreams he'd come to me and literally wipe away all the stresses of the world. Bad memories were replaced with new visions of love. This was the life!

But soon I'd have to get back to reality. How I'd miss this little recluse, but I was also looking forward to going back to work soon and catching up with my friends. I loved my job and my friends were a lot of fun. I hadn't even told any of them about Paul yet. Would I mention the new man in my life? Or should I keep him all to myself? Since he was probably just an illusion, I opted to keep quiet.

I grabbed my iPod and stepped out onto the patio. It was another beautiful day, so I thought I'd chill out on the deck lounge and listen to music. The sun felt nice on my skin and a soft breeze was blowing the wind chimes just a little. I snuggled down, put my earplugs in and switched on my iPod, closing my eyes . . .

You make me feel so wonderful, I said, looking up at his angelic face. *Where did you come from?*

He smiled that beautiful smile of his.

I've always been with you, my love, always just a whisper away. I watch you from afar, making sure you are safe. You cannot see me, which is saddening. But you feel me, I know you do. That's enough for me for now, he answered. *When you are asleep and your mind is open I can come to you and show you my love. You feel my caresses and hear my voice. This is my time with you and I savour it more than you can imagine. I wait patiently for you to fall asleep, my darling, so I can show you what it is to be loved completely.*

He bent down and kissed me. I felt a wave of passion sweep over me.

I long for this too, my sweet, more than you know, I answered.

He picked me up in his arms and carried me inside. The bed cover felt cool compared to the warmth of the sun. I could feel his heart beating faster and his breathing was getting louder. My own heart was racing and, once again, my senses were alive. My insides ached for him, but he wasn't one for rushing. He gently teased me with his lips, his fingers and his tongue. Oh God, his tongue! He did amazing things with his tongue! I could hardly control myself. He was masterful at his art and knew exactly when to stop. He seemed to enjoy torturing me and making me beg. His skin was so soft and smooth and I loved the feeling of his naked torso brushing against mine. Everything about him was beautiful. When his hands touched me it was almost electric. No matter what part of me he touched I tingled all over. Nothing or no one had ever made me feel this way. I wanted him now like I'd never wanted anything in my life.

He moved up closer to me, positioning his body above me as if reading my mind.

My eyes must have been pleading with him.

Yes, I am ready!!!!

He paused . . .

I heard a crow squawk and woke with a start, once again lying outside on the deck lounge with my iPod.

"Damn it!" I cursed. "Stupid bird!

I felt frustrated and annoyed. I tried to get back to sleep but was too wound up and couldn't relax.

Oh well, to be continued tonight, I thought to myself.

I decided a cold swim was in order!

Chapter 6
Mirage

Jenny kept looking at the clock. God, it was quiet tonight! She should have closed up early but needed this business to do well. She was really putting in the hours now. She had always been a talented designer and decided to open her own boutique. It was doing quite well, but she needed that big break before making her first million.

9 p.m.! Finally she could close up and head home. She'd been working all week and was looking forward to a hot bath and a glass of wine.

She punched the numbers into the alarm pad and quickly went out the door, locking it behind her. Her car was just across the road, which was good because the street was pretty deserted now. She started to walk across and then noticed the man. He was standing in the alley just back a bit from her car. Her heart started thumping. *God, what to do now?* She could go back into the shop and wait until he'd gone. Or maybe she should just get her keys ready and enter the car as quickly as possible, locking the doors straight away? She decided on the latter— a decision she regretted almost immediately.

He lunged at her as soon as she neared her car, grabbing her from behind and putting a knife to her throat. She was so scared she forgot all about her self-defense training. She couldn't see his face but knew he was white from his arm.

He never said a word, dragging her into the alley while holding the knife close to her throat. Her mind was racing.

God, please don't let him rape me or kill me! She silently pleaded.

She told him she had money in her purse, hoping this was just a mugging. But as soon as she opened her mouth he pushed the blade harder into her skin.

Panicked, she tried to struggle. This made him angry and he threw her onto the ground. She hit her head hard on the pavement and started to feel groggy.

As he tried to remove her underwear, she fought weakly. His strength overwhelmed her easily and he pinned her down with one arm while removing her panties with the other. She felt dizzy and nauseas. She knew she was going to die. He started to remove his own pants. She knew what was coming and was helpless to stop it. Her head wound seeped blood onto the concrete and she could feel the world fading away.

Why was this happening now just as she was starting to get her life together? She was a good person . . . why didn't God stop this from happening?

Please, please don't let him rape me, she begged inside her head.

Something moved in her peripheral vision then suddenly vanished. Her assailant disappeared. She could hear a man screaming and what sounded like an animal growling and hissing. Too disoriented to realise what was happening around her, she went numb. Nothing mattered except the rapist didn't return. There was crashing and banging and what sounded vaguely like slurping.

After what seemed like an eternity, Jenny felt herself being picked up and carried in strong arms. These were not the arms of her assailant, but rather comforting arms. She no longer felt in danger and knew, somehow, that she was safe and protected. She'd been spared and someone— or something— was now telling her she'd be okay. *Just hang in there,* said a voice, *and you'll be fine.*

The next thing she remembered was waking up in the hospital.

Nana sat staring at the computer screen.

"I wish these darn people would write in capitals or in a bigger font so I could bloody well read what they're trying to tell me!" She sighed. She had spent the evening trying to upload photos onto one of her many web pages, in between reading emails and messages from friends. Her eyes were getting tired and she was starting to see double.

"Oh well, Freddie, time to shut you down and try to catch up on some much needed sleep."

She knew sleep would probably elude her as it usually did when her mind was racing. But she needed to at least try. Even a few hours would do her some good.

The computer screen went black and she stood up, stretching her aching back. Sitting hunched over a computer screen wasn't exactly good for her arthritis, but she loved interacting with people. It could get very lonely in this big old house. Her husband had died a long time ago and her only son had disappeared. Nana and her daughter had searched and searched long after the cops had given up. She just didn't believe he was dead. She thought she would feel it if he was.

She pushed the chair in and walked down the hallway.

The young man waited outside in the shadows for the woman inside to go to bed.

I thought these old ducks went to bed early? He thought to himself, annoyed.

It was already after 1 a.m. and he'd been waiting for what seemed like an eternity.

He didn't want to hurt her. He just needed to get in and get out quickly, grab whatever crap was easy to hock off or swap for drugs. Laptops, cameras, mobile phones, etc — all were used as currency in the drug world, almost as good as cash. He could see her handbag sitting right there on the table. Very helpful!

Finally the light went out. He'd been casing her house out for the last few nights trying to figure a way in without making too much noise. He was pretty sure he'd found it. The cat door wasn't too far away from the door lock and she always left her keys dangling. He grabbed one of the bamboo stakes out of her garden and carefully maneuvered it through the cat door and into the key ring. The trick now was not to pull the keys out too fast and have them fall on the floor. The last thing he wanted to do was wake up the old biddy.

Very slowly and carefully, he pulled the keys out of the lock and lowered them down and through the cat door. Mission accomplished! Now he just had to unlock the door and he was in!

It always made it easier when they didn't have a dog. He was scared of dogs and always avoided those houses.

He quietly made his way over to the table. He could see her handbag clearly. Opening it, he peered inside. Jackpot! Purse, camera and mobile! This would do just nicely. There wasn't a lot of cash, but combined with the other goodies this haul would do just fine.

Now to get out of here.

Nana crept up behind the thief. She could hear her heart beating in her ears and was positive he must be able to hear it, too. She knew she should just let him take her handbag and not try and stop him. But that money had to last her until next pension day and the camera had pictures of her grandchildren she hadn't yet downloaded. She kept a mini baseball bat under her pillow and was going to knock him out with it! She had already dialed 000 and left the phone off the hook. Hopefully the cops were on the way.

He turned around just in time to see the baseball bat coming down and ducked. It smacked onto his shoulder and he cried out in pain, dropping the handbag on the floor. Out spilled the contents.

"What did you do that for, you stupid bitch? All I wanted was the fucking handbag! You should've just let me take it!" he yelled. Losing control, he struck her across the head, sending her reeling backwards.

"I didn't want to hurt you, I just need the money!"

"You need money for what, drugs? Then why don't you get a job and stop stealing off people who actually need that money to survive? This is what I need to eat for the next two weeks!" she yelled back.

He was getting angry now. He hadn't wanted a confrontation, just a quiet slip in and out. Then he'd be off to get his fix. He didn't need this sob story bullshit!

"Look lady, just stay out of my way. I'm taking your money and that's that. Not a damn thing you can do about it!"

He knelt down, picked up the handbag and started piling everything back into it. The old bitch had seen him now . . . and that wasn't part of the plan. What if she'd already rung the cops? He really had to get off this shit as it was turning him into a thief and woman basher.

"Just one more hit," he said out loud. "I'll give it up after that."

The addict didn't see the figure lurking in the shadows, watching and waiting.

Looking down at the bag and not watching where he was going, he walked smack into what felt like a brick wall.

"Fuck!" He said rubbing his head. He lifted his head and came eye to eye with a monster.

His jaw dropped and his eyes opened wide. He froze.

It was about 6 feet tall with long dark hair that was matted to its head. Its eyes were piercing blue, almost white. Fangs protruded from its mouth. It was covered from head to toe in blood and looking right at him . . . growling.

He tried to move but the monster grabbed him with a clawed hand and effortlessly lifted him off the ground.

Nana was peeking around the corner. She stifled a scream and froze, horrified but intrigued.

"Give the lady back her handbag," it snarled. "Give up the drugs, get a job, and stop stealing from innocent people. Or I WILL be back, comprendo? You're very lucky that I've already eaten tonight."

The addict nodded his head vigorously.

"Y-Yeah, sure I will," he stuttered.

The thing threw him against the fence. He fell to the ground hard. It looked at him and hissed. He threw the bag on the ground and limped off as fast as he could go.

It turned around and saw Nana watching. She ducked back around the corner hoping it hadn't spotted her. Her breathing was getting laboured and she realised her inhaler was in her handbag.

"Maybe it's gone," she thought to herself.

She slowly crept back round the corner and came face to face with it.

Gasping, she stepped back. It walked towards her. She didn't know what to do. She certainly couldn't outrun it.

Something in its stature seemed familiar and its eyes seemed almost sad. She didn't feel afraid anymore and sensed it was here to help her.

It bent down, picked up the handbag, and handed it to her. Then she thought it tried to smile, but it looked more like a grimace with teeth covered in blood. It opened its mouth as if to say something when the sound of sirens interrupted.

The knock on the door gave Nana a start and she spun round. She turned back to thank the thing for helping her, but it was gone.

He hung his head sadly. He had wanted to tell her, but how could he? It was obvious that she was terrified of him. She shied away from him and stared at him as if he was a monster.

That was his life now, scaring people. He was destined to live in the shadows, away from the light, hiding where people couldn't see his face. It was a fate worse than death, never again to be surrounded by loved ones or friends. He was hideous.

A Monster.

Even his own mother hadn't recognised him!

Chapter 7
Back to Reality

It felt strange coming back to Ellenbrook. I was apprehensive to go inside, not wanting the sadness over Paul to ruin my mood. I need not have worried— it felt like home. I unpacked, tackled a load of washing, and put the jug on. Coffee. What an awesome time I'd had at the beach house, not to mention the nights with the man I dreamt of every time I closed my eyes. Now I was looking forward to going back to work tomorrow. I couldn't wait catch up with my best friend Maria, who was a bit of a gossip but a lot of fun. I felt bad I hadn't rung her when Paul left. She'll chastise me, but I know she'll understand. I stirred my coffee and sat on the couch to drink it. Millions of thoughts whirled through my head. I wondered how He came to be in my dreams and if He was real. If He was real, how did He leave my fantasies and enter my reality?

I finished my coffee and ran a bath, looking forward to a nice long soak before bed. I wanted to join my lover once again. He was right. I did feel him around me all the time. Since the day my parents died I felt protected and safe. I never really understood why. Was he my Guardian Angel? He couldn't be an angel; angels surely didn't do what he did in my dreams! I knew now I hadn't imagined him. He was too real for even my vivid imagination. Tonight I would ask him more questions about what he was and where he came from. If he allows it, that is. He has a certain way of shutting me up.

I must have dozed off in the bath. He was there kissing me with those soft moist lips. Not only did he have the face of an angel, but the body and voice of one too. He handed me a towel and helped me out of the bath.

I'm sorry about what happened with Paul, he said genuinely. *I hate to see you sad.*

I'm not sad anymore, thanks to you, I smiled back at him, wrapping the towel around me and starting to walk out of the bathroom. He grabbed my arm and pulled me to him, kissing me passionately. I felt as if I'd faint— the feelings were that intense. My head was spinning and I pulled away from him, needing to lie down. I walked towards the bedroom and turned around to see if he was following me.

Are you coming? I asked, dropping the towel and letting it fall to the ground.

I will be very soon, he said with a cheeky grin, picking me up and tossing me onto the bed.

There was no gentle foreplay this time, just a sense of urgency and incredible excitement that totally consumed us. It was over as quickly as it begun and I was left gasping for air and in need of another bath.

Are you my Guardian Angel? I asked him. He bowed his head and looked troubled.

No, far from an angel. More like a monster, I'm afraid.

He looked at me with sadness in his eyes. He gave me half a smile then looked away.

I looked at this beautiful creature standing before me. A monster? He was in no way a monster. In fact, he was the most beautiful thing I'd seen in my life.

He looked puzzled. *Is it not enough that we have what we have? Do you need more?*

For now it's enough, my gorgeous man, but one day I'd like to hold you and be with you for real, not just in my dreams. Could it be possible, or are you destined to be only my dream lover? I waited, looking into his eyes.

I fear if you knew the truth, my love, you'd never forgive me and would no longer want me in your life. The things I do to survive are monstrous, although I've tried to be noble. One day, I fear, you will learn the truth and then I'll lose you forever . . .

The phone was ringing and I jumped out of the bath. Wrapping the towel around me I ran to the phone. It was Maria, asking if I'd be back tomorrow. It was good to hear her voice again, although the words I'd just heard a few minutes ago were still ringing in my head. I doubt anything he could have done would cause me not to want him anymore. So strong were my feelings for him, so deep was my passion. I felt I could forgive him anything as long as he came back to me.

Maria raved on about her latest conquest. Should I tell her about mine? Maybe I should keep him to myself just a little longer, although the compulsion to share was strong.

Soon I was pulling my jeep into the hospital car park. It felt like I'd been away for months, not merely two weeks. Maria spotted me the minute I arrived at reception and ran up to give me a big hug.

"Welcome back, girl. You won't believe what's been going on since you left!" She started going on about who was sleeping with who and the latest scandals. I smiled.

"Paul left me two weeks ago."

She stopped dead in her tracks and stared into my eyes with compassion.

"Are you alright?"

"I'm fine," I said, actually meaning it.

She looked puzzled.

"Two weeks ago and I am hearing about it now? What happened? What have you been doing the last two weeks?"

I spent the next hour in between patients and duties telling her how Paul had suddenly decided he didn't love me anymore. I explained that he'd left the first day of my holidays. I told her I'd gone away to the beach house to recoup and figure out what to do with the rest of my life. Now I was all healed and refreshed and ready to take on the world again. I think she was a little skeptical, suspecting that I may be hiding an aching heart. But eventually she seemed to accept it.

"Did you hear about last night?" Maria asked as we sat down to lunch at the hospital cafeteria. "The Ghost struck again."

The Ghost was the name the detectives had given to the serial killer who'd been murdering child molesters and rapists for the last 20 years, never leaving the slightest bit of evidence to help the police catch him. He seemingly got in and out through locked doors and windows, leaving no trace of ever being there. I didn't care if he never got caught. He was somewhat of a hero in my mind.

"No, I haven't heard the news this morning. What happened?"

"They found a man's mangled body in a dumpster in one of the alleys in the city. DNA identified him as a rapist cops have been trying to catch for months."

Good, I thought to myself. *Got what he deserved*

"Actually, one of the rapist's victims is in this hospital. She turned up at the hospital not knowing how she got here. She remembers the rapist was about to assault her, and then waking up in hospital. One of the orderlies found her on the front steps. Tests showed she wasn't raped, but she has quite a bad head injury."

There was something familiar about this story. A lot of women over the past 20 years had told similar tales. They, too, thought of the Ghost as a hero. Not only had he saved them from being raped, but most likely saved their lives, as well. As for the perpetrators being murdered . . . that was karma as far as I was concerned. Of course, the cops still had to try to find him. Vigilantes were criminals in the eyes of the law, even though most of the police force probably secretly sang his praises. He was helping to rid the streets of filth and saving many innocent people in the process.

I decided to visit this latest victim during my rounds. Her records identified her as Jenny. She was looking well and propped up on her pillows watching Days of our Lives on TV. I asked if she minded telling me what had happened. She didn't mind at all, so happy she was not to have been raped and murdered!

"I remember him holding a knife to my throat and then throwing me onto the ground. I hit my head really hard and almost blacked out. He was going to rape me," Jenny's voice quivered. She paused.

"But then suddenly he wasn't there anymore and I felt strong arms pick me up. The next thing I remembered was waking up here."

She looked at me and smiled.

"You didn't see the man who saved you?" I asked. I was really curious about this Ghost.

"No, but I felt him," she answered. "He was very warm and strong and I felt safe with him. It's hard to believe he's the same man ripping criminals apart. I'm forever indebted to him. If the cops do find him he should get a medal!"

I had to admit I agreed with her. This man intrigued me. He turned up in time to stop a horrendous crime and then went about killing the assailant, sparing future victims. The cops said in a few press conferences that the perpetrators were ripped apart as if by some sort of wild animal, impossible for a man to do. There was hardly any blood at the scene and no trace evidence at all. They were baffled and couldn't explain it.

Keep up the good work, was all I could think. *Hope they never catch you.*

The rest of the day pretty much went without incidence. I was a little tired coming back after such a relaxing break. My feet hurt.

"Drinks after work," Maria announced.

Darn! I was hoping to sneak out undetected. I wanted to get home to bed and my dark haired man. No chance of that now.

"Okay Maria, your place? I'll grab a bottle of wine on the way."

She smiled and nodded. Maybe I could have a quick drink and then get home to . . . dream.

"Where's the corkscrew?" I was looking in the drawer where it usually was, but couldn't see it.

"Right in front of you, I'm sure you need glasses, woman!" Maria laughed as she picked it up out of the drawer and handed it to me.

She was a beautiful woman with long red hair and sparkling green eyes. Her smile lit up any room and she certainly had her share of admirers. She wasn't ready to settle down and start making babies just yet. She was "still having fun," as she put it. I opened the bottle, poured us both a generous glass, and headed over to sit beside her on the couch.

"So tell me about what's been happening," she said, smiling at me and sipping from her glass.

I retold the story of Paul, in more detail this time. Years ago I told her of a man I dreamt of every night. She'd been very interested and always pried me for details. But there had never really been many details to share . . . until Paul left. My dark haired man had only held me and soothed me before. But with Paul gone I was free, and my dream lover knew it.

"How on earth did you get through that without even so much as a phone call to your best friend?" she asked. "You know I'd have called in my sick leave and come with you to the beach house for a few days, better than you moping there all alone."

I looked at her and smiled.

"I wasn't exactly alone," I replied. "Technically, but not really."

She looked at me as if I had lost my mind.

"What do you mean?"

"He was with me," I said blushing and looking down at my glass.

At first I could see it didn't register, but then it clicked. She realized who the "He" was.

"Oh, what did he do? Tell me everything!"

And so I did.

Starting from the fall from the balcony to the amazing lovemaking, I poured out the details. She sat listening intently, gasping and grabbing my arm when I got to the juicy bits. At least she wasn't looking at me like I was a crazy woman, even though she was convinced I'd made him up.

"Give me some of that," she laughed. "You lucky thing, imagine going to bed every night to that?"

"I don't have to imagine," I said smiling.

"Wow, maybe you knew him in another life or maybe he is a dream man that you've invented until you find one for real?"

I had no idea, but I was very glad he was here. We spent the rest of the night talking about possible reasons for him coming to me and the latest man in Maria's sights. It was fun. I ended up enjoying myself and was glad I went.

I was so tired when I got home that I kicked off my shoes and lay on top of my bed, asleep in no time.

I woke to the alarm in the morning, still fully dressed and feeling confused. *He didn't come to me last night. Why, after all these wonderful nights, did he not show? Was I not supposed to tell anyone? But I'd told Maria before about him, although not in such detail . . . Or was it the questions I asked him last night? Had I scared him off?* I got up feeling a genuine sense of loss and sadness. I climbed into the shower and let the water run over me.

Please come back to me, I begged.

Chapter 8
A Dream Come True

But he didn't come back.

The next few weeks went by without as much as a sign. I'd had him in my life for the last 16 years, so his absence left a huge hole. I tried to act normal at work and around Maria, but inside I was dying. He'd promised he would never leave me . . . but he had. I don't know why I was so upset, considering he wasn't even real. But I felt like I'd lost my soul mate. I wasn't sleeping well, and it was showing. I was tired all the time and really not feeling myself at all.

"Are you going to eat that?" Maria asked. "You've been staring into space for the last ten minutes."

"I'm not really hungry," I said looking down at my plate of macaroni cheese.

"Cool," she said and grabbed it off my plate, shoveling it into her mouth.

God knows how she stayed so slim. The woman ate like a horse. As I watched her wolfing down my lunch, my stomach started to churn. Great! On top of everything, now I have food poisoning. I ran to the toilet and only just made it before throwing up the little bit I'd managed to eat.

Why is the universe doing this to me? I'm a good person. Haven't I had enough heartache for one lifetime? I felt better after ridding myself of my stomach contents and went back out to warn Maria. Too late. She'd just finished the last spoonful. *Better not tell her,* I thought, *or she'll will herself into being sick, as well!*

"Are you okay, Hun, you look a little pale?"

"Yes, just a bit of a funny tummy. Probably something I ate," I said, looking at the empty plate and smiling.

She glanced down at my lunch which she'd just devoured.

"Nah probably just that time of month," she said, smiling and oblivious. "Let's get out of here."

We went outside into the fresh air to enjoy our last fifteen minutes of freedom. It was another beautiful sunny day, so we decided to soak up some free vitamin D while it lasted. I recalled what Maria had said. When was I due? With all that had been going on, I'd completely lost track of my cycle. She was probably right, though. I'd been feeling tired and I did get a queasy stomach just before getting my period. And I didn't feel sick now, so it couldn't be food poisoning. Hopefully I had some tampons in my handbag just in case it decided to come while I was still at work.

I walked inside to a quiet house. It really did seem empty now that my friend was no longer present. I had to figure out how to keep going without him. It would be hard, but I had to do it.

Coffee and a bath, think about dinner later. I turned the taps to run a bath then put the kettle on. I made my coffee and went back to check the water temperature—perfect. I grabbed the coffee and thought I'd have it in the bath. Multitasking! I climbed in . . . heaven. A good soak is just what I needed after today. I went to take a sip of coffee and my stomach churned. *Not again!* I really started to feel sick and jumped out of the bath, running to the toilet to once again throw up. This time I felt really ill, literally sitting on the floor retching and hugging the toilet. *Great. I really am sick.* I wrapped the towel around me and lay down on my bed. I was asleep almost immediately.

I woke in the morning feeling a little better . . . until I stood up. Immediately I was back to hugging the toilet again. I rang work and told them I had food poisoning or a stomach bug and wouldn't be in today. Maria rang a little while later.

"Do you need anything, Hun? It couldn't be the mac cheese, coz I'm fine. Maybe you should do a pregnancy test?"

"What? No, I can't be pregnant! Paul and I always used protection."

"But what about your mystery man, did you use protection with him?" she said, laughing.

"Honestly, Hun, you're a nurse. You know that nothing but abstinence is 100%."

She was right. I'd been tired and vomiting and God knows if my period was overdue or not. Just great, wouldn't that just be my luck? The guy knocks me up and then leaves me because he doesn't want to have kids. Or maybe . . . ? No! That was crazy! My dark haired man wasn't real and unless this was a phantom pregnancy, it would have to be Paul's. That was, if I was pregnant at all.

The chemist was really busy and I was having trouble finding the home pregnancy tests. I finally grabbed one and took it to the counter. Why did I feel so self-conscious? It wasn't like I was doing anything wrong, but I felt almost guilty as if everyone was looking at me. God, I was 33, not 15, so why was this such a big deal? No one here even knew me.

I took the test out of the box and read the instructions. I'd never taken a pregnancy test before. Okay, pee on the end bit, put the cap on . . . and wait. The results should show within three minutes. That was easy enough. The plus sign came up almost immediately. Positive. *God what was I going to do now?* I couldn't tell Paul. I'd just gotten over him and he'd made it quite clear he didn't want children. Could I do this myself? I was scared, but also a little excited. I'd always wanted kids and by a strange twist of fate, I was finally going to be a mother. I put my hand on my stomach.

"My baby," I whispered. *Yes, I could do this.*

Chapter 9
Recurring Dreams

"It was positive. I'm pregnant.

"Maria stared at me in disbelief.

"Oh my God, Hun, are you okay? What are you going to do? Have you told Paul?"

"I'm fine Maria. And no, I'm not going to tell Paul."

I put my hand on my stomach and smiled.

"This is my baby. He didn't want kids remember? I can do this myself. My parents left me enough money and I can support myself. I don't need a man."

It wasn't entirely true. I missed my dream lover so much, but knowing now I had a child growing inside me helped somewhat to ease the pain. I didn't feel so alone anymore. I thought constantly about my pregnancy. I'd wanted a baby so much with Paul . . . but he obviously didn't reciprocate those feelings. And so he left me. Now I was pregnant and felt as if I'd been given a second chance. I was going to grab it with both hands! Destiny—that is what it was.

Maria didn't seem convinced and looked at me as if I was crazy. Unlike me, she wasn't the least bit maternal and could think of nothing worse than having a snot nosed brat running around. We talked a bit more and then Maria left me with my thoughts. I felt content and in control, convinced I could do this on my own.

I daydreamed about my dark haired man holding our baby and smiling, of the two of us cuddling and kissing and watching our baby sleeping. Walking down the street pushing the pram, going to the park, making love . . . *how perfect it would be if he was real. What would I do if he was real?*

Of course, he wasn't. I couldn't go through life living in a dream world. I had to snap out of it and start thinking about me and my baby. I needed to focus on what was real.

Tomorrow was late night shopping in the city, so I decided to start looking at things for the nursery. Yes, it was a bit early to start shopping for the baby, but looking and planning couldn't hurt. It gave me something else to focus on instead of . . . Him. Him with his dreamy eyes and gorgeous smile, I could picture him now, so beautiful. If I closed my eyes, I could feel him close, breathing on my neck. I could feel his arms around my waist. *God, I wanted him back. How could he leave me like this?*

I decided to go to bed. Who was I kidding? I couldn't get him out of my head if I tried. We were connected somehow and deep in my soul I was sure he was real. How could he not be? I could still feel him and smell him. Everywhere I went I felt him close. It was so unfair. He left my dreams but was still haunting me, invisible arms embracing me and invisible lips kissing my neck. *How can I forget you when you won't let me?* I lay on my bed and started to sob. I was so confused. Was I losing my mind?

I'm sorry you're sad, whispered a familiar voice. *I left because I think maybe I'm doing more harm than good. I've always been present, helping you when your parents died. Then again, when your boyfriend left. But now I know we could never be. This is no life for you and you could never love me if you knew what I was . . . knew the truth.*

He was suddenly beside me, head in his hands and looking so sad. My heart ached and I wanted so badly to hold him and say it was okay. I would always love him, no matter what. But something in his tone disturbed me and I wondered what this big secret was. How could he be anything but good? He was so loving and kind, not to mention drop dead gorgeous! I stood up and wrapped my arms around his neck, declaring my feelings.

I love you and I think we both know that I can't go back. I can't forget you and move on . . . you are part of me now.

He raised his head and looked into my eyes. I melted inside. There was such sorrow in his look, mixed with longing. Longing to be loved. Longing to be accepted. I could see the inner turmoil. He wanted so much to love me but was afraid—afraid of what that would mean.

Please, I begged, burying my head into his chest. *Don't leave me again. I cannot bear to be without you!*

He looked utterly dejected and said, *My heart is breaking, but it could never work. We're from different worlds and we don't fit into each other's lives. I can't come into yours and I could never ask you to be part of mine.*

Don't shut me out! Please let me in! I cried. *Don't you understand? I need you. You've been with me through every tragedy in my life, since I was 17. How could I live without you now?*

I've been around longer than that, he said. *We're linked you and I, and I don't know how to break the chain that connects us. But I must try, or I fear you'll be destroyed by what you find.*

He turned to walk away, but I grabbed him and flung myself against him. I didn't understand. He obviously loved me, so why did he have to leave? Why couldn't he just tell me? He wrapped his arms around me and pulled me close, kissing my hair. I could hear his heart beating and lifted my head to look into his eyes. I think at that moment I knew I would forgive him anything if only he would kiss me. As if reading my thoughts again he bent his head and kissed me softly on the lips.

I will always love you, he said. *It's a matter of being cruel to be kind, so to speak. There are things about me you cannot know. I'm destined to be alone for ever.*

He moved his hand to my stomach and smiled.

I've given you a gift my love. Please do not blame this child for what his father has become. Do not let the sins of the father fall onto his son. For he is innocent like you.

The alarm in my queasy belly went off. Great timing, as usual. I got out of bed and stumbled to the bathroom. *What did he mean? How could he possibly be this baby's father?* It made me a darn sight happier to think of him as the father than Paul. *Quick shower, breakfast and then off to work.* How I was going to concentrate at work today was beyond me!

Chapter 10
Rude Awakenings

I was still feeling a little queasy but found that ginger and vitamin B6 eased it a little. I arrived at work five minutes late and got a scowl from the Ward Sister. Apologising, I quickly put my bag in the smoko room and headed back to the Nurse's Station.

"How are you today?" Maria looked at me with real concern in her face. "Try not to overdo things, okay?"

I smiled.

"I'll be fine, don't worry."

"Okay," she said, still looking as if she didn't quite believe me. "Jenny is going home today."

I wanted to see her before she left. Something about Jenny's story seemed so familiar and I thought maybe if I talked to her some more it might shed some light on why. I assigned myself to be her "checking out" person and headed off to see her.

She was happy to be going home.

"How are you today?" I asked. "Have you organised someone to pick you up later?"

She smiled and nodded. "My mum will be here after lunch. I feel so happy to be alive, you know, and it's all thanks to the Ghost. I honestly hope the police never figure out where he came from."

I agreed. The Ghost was doing a good job at cleaning up the streets. Jenny seemed so happy now, especially knowing the man who had attacked her was dead and no longer a threat.

"I owe him my life, not to mention stopping that man from . . . " She stopped and looked at me.

There was no need to say the words. As women, we both knew the fear of being raped.

"For some reason, Jenny, I have a feeling of de javu when you tell your story. I'm not sure why, but I have this niggling deep down that I've heard or seen something to do with this guy."

"Maybe he saved you in another life?" she said. She wasn't smiling and stared at me, quite serious.

"Maybe," I said.

I got all the paperwork sorted and said goodbye, giving Jenny a hug and wishing her luck before I left.

I was very curious about her case. Why I felt so connected to it, I wasn't sure. Maybe it was the fact that I'd survived a crash and, like Jenny, ended up at this hospital with no explanation of how I got here. Did the Ghost have something to do with saving me from the car accident that killed my parents? Now I was getting curious.

I went to the file room and found Jenny's records. I read her statements about the attack and her account of blacking out and waking up at the hospital, so similar to my own experiences. I couldn't remember the car accident and only recalled waking up in this very same hospital. I wonder? I started to search for my own file. I read about how I had no next of kin as both my parents were deceased, and how the hospital staff had found me on the front steps, unconscious.

Hang on a minute . . . there was another page in here. But I couldn't remember ever being in hospital before. It was 20 years ago. How could I not know about this? I began reading the page.

"Repeatedly raped, strangled by stepfather . . ."

This couldn't be me! I never had a stepfather and I'd never been raped or strangled! But the document had my name on it and date of birth. I stared at the page in disbelief. What the hell was going on?

Chapter 11
Past Life

My head was spinning. What was going on? I'd never been "almost" murdered and my parents had still been happily married and together when they died. It must be a mistake. Yet my name and birth date were accurate and deep inside me I knew something wasn't right. How could I find out now? Both my parents were dead. I kept staring at the paper in front of me. It couldn't be me. Surely I'd remember something so horrible happening in my childhood? I tried to think, but my ears were ringing and I had to sit down. Could it be me? How could I not know about this? How could I have been raped and strangled and have no memory of it? I felt dizzy and numb all over. Had my parents broken up at one stage? Had mum remarried, this time to a monster? None of this made any sense. One thing was certain, though. I was damn well going to find out!

"What's this?' Maria asked me when I handed her the file at lunch.

"It's my file," I said.

She frowned and opened it.

"What do you mean your file? From when you were in the accident? Why would you want to dredge all that up again, Hun? Nothing good can come of looking at things so morbid."

She had that worried look on her face, one I'd seen so many times over the past few weeks.

"Read it," I said sternly, picking up my coffee and taking a sip.

She looked at me, realizing I was deadly serious. She started to read the paper in front of her—the one from many years earlier when I'd been sexually abused and strangled by a stepfather who didn't exist. She read in total silence, then looked up at me with horror in her eyes.

"This can't be right! You had a wonderful childhood and your parents surely would have told you if anything like this had happened?"

"That's what I thought at first, too, but look at the name and birth date. I'm going to investigate, Maria. I have to know the truth."

For once in her life Maria was speechless. The silence seemed to last for ages until finally she broke it.

"You should ask Moyra. She's worked at this hospital for over 20 years. A case like this would surely stick in her mind. She might remember something."

I jumped up from the table and ran over to Maria, giving her a big hug and kissing her on the cheek.

"What a great idea! Why didn't I think of that? Moyra would certainly remember, and we know what a big gossip she is. She won't be able to keep it to herself. Oh thank you Maria, I knew you'd help me!"

I grabbed my file, kissed her again and ran off to find Moyra and continue my quest for answers.

Chapter 12
Retracing Steps

No one really knew exactly how old Moyra was. She'd been at this hospital for as long as any of us could remember and had to be in her late 50s, if not older. She held her age well, though, and although a lot of us hazarded guesses, none of us were brave enough to actually ask her. Her hair was long and dark and was only now starting to show slight streaks of grey. She had a lovely, friendly face and smiled a lot. On her frame were the biggest boobs I'd ever seen! She wasn't on the medical staff but worked in patient filing. If there were any major cases or gossip going on in the hospital, you could be sure Moyra knew about it.

I decided to approach her as if I was asking about someone other than myself. If she knew I was snooping into my own case file, she may be a little tight-lipped. If it was gossip about someone else, however, I was sure she'd freely spill the beans.

"Hello love, what brings you here?" she asked in her lovely English accent, peering over top of her glasses. Her big brown eyes sparkled as she smiled at me.

"Hi Moyra, I was wondering if you could help me with an old patient note I found. I came across it this morning and wondered if you remembered anything about it. It was a young girl who'd been sexually abused by her stepfather. He tried to strangle her. She was brought to this hospital about twenty years ago and I wondered if you were here then?"

She wrinkled her brow and pursed her lips searching her thoughts.

"Oh yes," she replied, "I remember that. She was in a coma for a while. When she woke up she couldn't remember anything about the attack or anything about the last few years. Very traumatic for the poor wee thing, and to think it was the fault of her own mother to leave her with that awful man! Poor girl had been abused as well, and her mother had no idea until the hospital informed her."

I shuddered. Had my mother left me to be abused and tortured by some maniac? It sure didn't sound like the mother I knew and loved.

"Do you remember anything else, Moyra?" I asked, trying not to look too eager. My hands were trembling and I stuck them into my pockets, trying to look as natural as possible.

Moyra seemed a little suspicious now.

"Why do you ask, Petal? Do you know her or something?"

"Just curious after seeing the note, that's all," I said trying to look convincing. "Thanks for the info, Moyra," I said with a tight smile as I headed back to the wards.

"There was something about her raving about a Guardian Angel when they first brought her in," she shouted after me.

I kept walking and waved over my shoulder.

"Thanks, talk to you soon." I could feel her eyes watching me as I turned the corner.

Okay, so now what do I do? Moyra pretty much confirmed what I'd read, and now I needed to do a little research to confirm if the young victim was actually me . . . but where to start? Births, Deaths and Marriages would show if mum and dad had divorced and whether or not she remarried.

Maybe I could Google my story and see what came up. So many questions swirled round and round in my head. I had to find out and sooner rather than later. I decided to nip into the library during my break and have a quick look at the Internet.

3 p.m. seemed to drag, but finally I was able to get to a computer. I typed in "young girl strangled by stepfather" and was shocked at how many hits I got. Okay, so I'd have to narrow it down. I knew the year was around 1990 and I also typed in the name of the hospital.

This time I found it. I started to read one of the newspaper reports. It said a 13-year-old girl had been almost choked to death by her stepfather and was in a coma, later waking up with no memory of her attacker or the last two years. The assailant had later been found by police dead, literally ripped to pieces in his own car. There were no leads to whomever or whatever had done it and enquiries were still continuing. I looked at a few more, mostly the same. One, however, confirmed what Moyra had said about me ranting on about a Guardian Angel.

My break was up and I had to get back to work. Great, now I was left with even more questions. I would look online later, at home. I wondered what else I could find.

I was walking back to my car totally absorbed with my thoughts when suddenly someone ran up behind me and grabbed me round the shoulders. I got a fright until a familiar voice said, "Hi, I'm back. Did you miss me?"

"Of course I missed you, Hayley! When did you get back?"

She bounced around, smiling

"Late last night. I slept most of today but thought I'd try and catch up this arvo. What are you doing after work?"

Hayley was one of our midwives and I found her very easy to get on with. She was always smiling and happy, loved life, and totally enjoyed her job.

"Was thinking about doing some shopping . . . why? Did you want to come over for a chat and catch up?

"Definitely," she said literally beaming. "I'll grab us some champagne and sorbet and make some slushies."

"Better make it lemonade or non-alcoholic champers if you can find some. Don't want this kid coming out with FAS!"

She gasped.

"Oh you're not, are you?"

I nodded and smiled.

She was so excited she jumped up and down on the spot. I had to go back to work and asked her to meet me at home around 9 this evening. Then I could tell her everything. She hugged me again, kissed me on the cheek, and practically skipped off down the street. She always made me smile and I felt a little better as I drove back to the hospital.

Chapter 13
Your Worst Nightmare

The man sat in his car, waiting for her to appear. He'd been watching her from afar for a long time now. Recently she'd gone away for a while and he'd never found out where. He just knew she wasn't going to work every day as usual. He'd memorised her schedule and knew her shifts well. Now she was back, and he sat patiently waiting for her to get out of her car. He watched and waited, diligent and focused. He was drawn to her as he'd been to the others, but everything had to be perfect before putting his plan into action.

He'd taken his time with each one of them, but they'd all led to disappointment, all crying like pathetic little children for him to let them go. Not one of them could return the love he obviously possessed for them. He'd given them everything and still they did not love him or even appreciate him. For their disloyalty they'd paid the ultimate price—with their lives. Well, if he could not have their unconditional love he didn't see why any other man should, either.

Yes, he would make the perfect husband and worship the ground she walked on. All he'd expect in return was her total devotion to him in the bedroom. It wasn't too much for a man to ask from his wife. After all, wasn't it her duty to satisfy his every sexual need? The others had all been prudes and weren't willing to even try to please him.

"Why do they always shy away from me in disgust?" he wondered.

He was a good looking man who had a healthy sexual appetite and needed a woman who understood this. So far he hadn't found "The One." They cowered and begged him not to hurt them. It wasn't as if they were virginal and unaccustomed to the touch of a man. He had surveilled their exploits and conquests well before even taking them on their first date.

He knew how a woman should be treated. He would certainly shower his newest love interest with gifts, cook a beautiful meal with expensive wine, and set a romantic scene. Oh, he'd spare no expense and show her what being with him could be like. The others always whinged and moaned about going home without making an effort to reciprocate his feelings. Once in the bedroom they were totally clueless as to how to please their man. Surely this time would be different?

Once his conquests stepped foot into his love room they'd become hysterical and try to escape. He'd have to restrain them and tape their mouths shut to stop the screaming and struggling. He only wanted to teach them how to do it properly. No pain no gain, wasn't that the motto? Well, he'd certainly shown them the pain but had so far fallen short on the gain.

True, they managed to get him in the mood but a few of them had died during the foreplay, well before he'd even finished his love making. Weak! How was he meant to finish when they went and died on him? He did prefer his woman to be moving and resorted to having sex with their lifeless bodies only out of necessity. Most, however, survived right to the end. Still, they lacked that certain something to leave him feeling fulfilled. Then afterwards they'd become babies, whimpering and pleading to be set free. Well he'd set them free, all right. They could swim with the fishes for all he cared. It was unbelievable how ungrateful they were, especially after learning what it meant to be made love to by a real man.

He hoped this one would live up to his expectations.

He knew she lived alone, as he'd followed her home a few times. It was obvious her boyfriend no longer lived there. She shouldn't be too hard to woo, and he'd start the courtship very soon. He started to feel himself stir and harden in anticipation. He could hardly wait! Maybe this one could please him the way he longed to be pleased. But he must be patient and make sure everything was as it should be, or his efforts would all be for nothing. Tomorrow she was on the afternoon shift and then off work for a few days. That's when he'd strike. No one would notice if she was away for a few days.

He watched her get out of her car and go into the hospital. God, she was beautiful . . . and soon she would be his. *Tomorrow, until tomorrow my love*. He could hardly contain himself!

Chapter 14
Disturbia

The excitement was mounting. Tonight was the night! The house was spotless and everything was prepared. He checked and double checked that everything was just right. It had to be perfect. She was the one . . . he was certain of it! She'd set him free from this relentless longing inside, this black hole that seemed to grow bigger and bigger with each failure. It needed to be filled and she'd be the one to do it.

Long ago he realised he wasn't like other men. He had needs, needs that far outweighed anything or anyone . . . needs that couldn't be satiated with just any woman. Only a special woman, strong yet yielding, could satisfy his hunger. His heart raced and butterflies fluttered in his stomach. Finally the day had come when she would be all his— his to do with whatever his heart desired. His heart desired a lot.

He walked into the bedroom, soundproofed with no windows. On the blood stained walls were pictures of his past loves in various stages of death. Some were only seconds gone, whereas others he'd kept until the smell was overpowering and he had to put them away and not play with them anymore. Sad, he did prefer live playmates, but sometimes desperation kicked in and he needed to finish the ritual. If they died too soon he was forced to continue as if they were still breathing.

But this one, she would be different. He knew in his heart she'd make it to the end and succumb to his charms. He had a lot of toys and looked at them all lovingly. They were all he had left until the right woman made it all complete. They were his family now, now that he had killed his whore of a mother and her bastard boyfriend. God, how he'd enjoyed it! They had made his life hell and he repaid the favour and made their deaths hell. He smiled thinking about it. They had been his firsts, but many more followed. All of them, of course, always begged for their pathetic lives. But fair is fair. After all, his parents hadn't listened when he begged not to be raped and beaten up as a child. Why would his victims expect any mercy from him? He'd inflicted unimaginable pain on them and found it such a turn on that it had become an addiction.

The search, he'd searched high and low for the woman to take away his pain. He knew he'd stop looking as soon as he found Mrs. Right. At this point, he was sure his search was now over.

His whole being ached for her, he was hard and eager to get started but knew he had to wait. *Be patient just a little while longer*. His hand slid into his pants, touching himself lovingly. He closed his eyes and slowly caressed himself. He wanted her now. It was so frustrating! Maybe he could just this once relieve himself beforehand. It felt so good and it was so hard. It was such a shame to waste it. *But no! It was too soon.* He opened his eyes and took his hand out of his pants. He tried to compose himself and check everything again. He must not ruin the thrill by pleasuring himself. Not when he would have her tonight.

"Soon my love, soon we will be together— at last. Until tonight," he said as he walked out of the bedroom, closing and locking the door behind him.

Chapter 15
Illusions

The last few hours dragged. My mind was miles away and definitely not focused on the job. I asked Maria if she wanted to join us after work, but she had a hot date and was going straight home to prepare the lair!

At last it was 8:30 p.m. I got out of the hospital as soon as I could and hurried home to find Hayley waiting in the driveway.

I told her about Paul and the pregnancy and what I'd found out today. After a few coffees and some intense discussion we decided to jump on the computer and Google. What else would we find out? It was nice to huddle with a partner in crime while I tried to determine if my whole life had been a lie.

We found my mother's marriage notice in the paper online. My heart sank. It was true. My mother and father had divorced and mum married a madman. We searched some more and found a story about my stepfather's murder. He had been found ripped apart inside his car with all the doors and windows locked. No wonder Jenny's story sounded familiar. Looks like the Ghost had saved me, too.

I was so confused. Why could I not remember any of this? There were more stories saying the police were puzzled as to how this guy got in and out without leaving any sign. All other similar cases had women saying they'd seen an angel just before they passed out. So far, he'd never been caught and was still ridding the streets of this filth to this day. I owed my life to him. But who was he and where did he come from? Words I had heard recently suddenly rang in my ears.

I recalled that my dark haired man had said, "I've been around you longer than that." Was it possible? Could the man I loved with all my heart be this vigilante? A killer of rapists and child molesters! But how could my sweet, lovely man possibly double as this murderer? Was my love actually someone who tore people apart with his bare hands and completely drained their bodies of blood? There was no logical explanation. But then nothing about this whole thing had anything to do with logic.

I must have been staring off out into space as I suddenly noticed Hayley's hand waving in front of my face.

"Hey, are you okay?" She said looking really concerned. "That is a hell of a lot to take in!"

"Yeah, I'm okay. I'm just thinking about the person who saved me that day, My Guardian Angel." I answered. I could feel my cheeks burning. Even suspecting that he might have been the person who tore others limb from limb. I still got a rush when I pictured him in my head.

"We have to find out more," said Hayley. "You need to know the whole story so you can get proper closure. Not just for your sake, but for the baby's sake as well."

Oh God, I suddenly remembered that he said the baby was his. What did that mean? Would my baby be like him, some sort of animal? What did he look like when he was ripping these men apart? Certainly not the vision of perfection I saw in my dreams, I was sure. *Was he a terribly ugly monster all covered in hair with red glowing eyes . . .?* A shiver went down my spine. No, he said the baby was like me, not him. A sense of relief rushed over me. Was I actually starting to believe that he was real? Not only that, but that the man of my dreams was actually the Ghost and that he hadn't aged a day after killing monsters over the last 20 years. The more I pondered, the more I became confused. Could he possibly be my baby's father, as well? How on earth was I ever going to get answers? I felt light headed and strange emotions were taking over me—horror, excitement, fear, hope and love. Yes love. I did love him. But then I had only seen the beautiful, gentle side of him . . . not his super human Jack the Ripper side!

I remembered his words. He said if I knew the truth, he'd lose me. Was that true? Could I let him touch me again knowing what he was? But then, I didn't exactly know what he was. It was quite obvious he wasn't an angel. So what was he, then?

"I think it's time I went," Hayley's voice broke the silence and my thoughts. "You obviously have a lot to think over."

She got up and took our glasses to the sink.

"I'm back at work Monday, so we can catch up at lunch or something. Text me if you need me, though."

I followed her outside and gave her a hug as she left. She was a good friend and I was so lucky to have people who cared about me. I stood out on the doorstep and waved as she drove off. I turned to walk back inside and heard a scuff behind me. Before I had the chance to turn around he had his hand and a cloth over my mouth. I could smell something strange. I started to panic as I realised it was chloroform, but could already feel myself slipping.

Then, for the third time in my life, everything went black.

Chapter 16
Delusions of Grandeur

I could hear music off in the distance. I couldn't quite make out the song, but it was a love song. I tried to open my eyes and move but everything felt so heavy, even though all my senses were starting to become aware. I remembered saying goodbye to Hayley but was having a hard time remembering what happened after that. Was I asleep? I didn't remember going to bed. I started to feel anxious. Where was I? Why couldn't I move and who was playing that music? I could hear a male voice humming along and some kitchen noises, range hood going and dishes clanking. It was slowly coming back to me. A hand had covered my mouth . . . and then nothing.

My mind was racing and I felt panicky, but I still couldn't move! I tried to calm myself down to think. Obviously someone had taken me, but why? What were they going to do to me? I was frightened and attempted to pull myself together. I tried desperately to move, but whatever drug he'd given me had paralysed everything but my mind. He was singing now. He sounded very happy, singing along about love and happiness.

God, he must be some kind of nutter, I thought to myself. *What am I going to do?*

I didn't have work today and no one was going to miss me. No one would even realise I was missing until Monday when I didn't show up for work!

"God, I hope my baby is alright," I thought to myself, and as if answering my question I felt a little flutter.

Thank you, God, I thought. *Now please help us to live through this.*

"She will wake up soon," he mused, savoring the power he had over her life. Everything was just about ready. A lovely beef casserole in the slow cooker, veggies done, and a decadent chocolate cake for dessert! The table was set and looked beautiful, filled with lovely scented candles and a favorite bottle of red wine. All it needed was the guest of honour, and she would be with us very soon. He felt a lump in his throat. She was so beautiful and tonight she would be his and his alone. After all, this time he'd finally found her. He wiped a tear from the corner of his eye.

"Soon, my love, we can begin our life together."

He walked over to the couch where she lay like a princess, so pretty in her little dress. He stroked her hair. It was silky and shiny and felt so lovely. He bent down to smell it and caught a scent, fruity and sweet. He touched her cheek. Her skin, so soft and smooth, accompanied a perfect nose and luscious lips. He had to kiss those lips. The suspense was killing him . . . just one taste. He gently touched his lips to hers and a shiver ran through him, soft and warm and full.

His eyes travelled down her body resting on her heavy breasts. They seemed bigger than he remembered but were still so beautifully formed. He traced the shape of them with his finger and then moved his hands down to her legs. Her skin was flawless and he felt so proud to have this woman as his own, softly running his hands up her leg to the edge of her dress. He had waited so long for her and he was literally aching for her now. His hand slid under her dress.

He could take her now while she was unconscious just once to ease the throbbing. He pondered on the thought for a while. He needed it so much, but it would ruin everything if he was to relieve himself now. The build-up was incredible and the release would be amazing once they were finally together. No, he would stick to the plan no matter how much he wanted to make love to her right there and then. Self-control was the key to true happiness and fulfillment. He stood up and walked back into the kitchen. Get your mind back on dinner. Dessert is for later!

Cassie was terrified. She could feel this stranger's hands touching her and felt him kiss her. *Please don't let him rape me or take my baby,* she thought. But he hadn't tried to rape her. He'd left again and gone back to the kitchen. What was he planning to do, then, and how was she going to escape? She could smell the food and had to admit she was starving. She hadn't been eating a lot lately and the lovely aromas coming from the kitchen mixed with fear had made her stomach feel very empty.

Her only chance was to go along with whatever little fantasy he'd cooked up. She wasn't strong enough to fight him off and would go along with it, all the while trying figure out a way out. She could move her toes! The drug must be starting to wear off. Her heart was pounding but she had to try and stay calm and clear headed if she was to get out of this alive.

Slowly her body was waking up. She could open her eyes, although she still felt really groggy. She lay there a while looking around the room. She was lying on a couch in a small room. She could see a kitchen with a man busily working away and to the left a small table and chairs with candles burning. The man had his back to her and she could see that he had blond hair and was tall and muscular. He was singing away and looked very domesticated with his apron on.

He turned and saw her looking at him. He clapped his hands together and smiled. He was very attractive with big blue eyes and a very white smile. He rushed over to where she was lying.

"You're finally awake!" He said sitting down beside her on the couch. "Hungry?" he asked, holding out one of his hands for her to take.

Cassie forced a smile.

"Starving," she said taking his hand and he beamed that beautiful smile back at her.

Cassie noticed that although his features were perfect and his eyes very blue and very pretty, there was nothing behind them. His smile never reached his eyes. She felt a shudder but let him lead her to the table. She was a little unsteady on her feet, but he held her up effortlessly and almost carried her to her seat. He was very strong and she knew it wouldn't be easy to escape.

"You sit here, my love, and I will go and get your dinner. Tonight you are my queen and I'm here to serve you," he announced gallantly, taking her hand, kissing it, and then heading back to the kitchen.

Cassie hoped like hell he was just some nut job who wanted a pretty dinner companion, but deep down she knew her life was in danger.

Just try and stay calm, she thought. *Don't show fear and maybe he won't attack . . . or did that tactic only work on wild animals?*

Her instincts told her that if she just kept her wits about her she would survive. *Humour him and let him wait on me, if that is what he wants.*

She was hungry after all!

Chapter 17
Dreams of a Future

Cassie still felt very weak and knew she wouldn't be anywhere strong enough to escape her captor. She was trying very hard to stay calm and in control. The slightest slip up and she knew things could become a whole lot worse. He was clearly insane and very handsome with almost perfect features, but not an inkling of an emotion showed anywhere on his face. Psychopath or sociopath? She wasn't sure of the correct term, but she knew he was one of those people who lacked a conscience and would murder his own grandmother without a second thought.

Her mind was still a little groggy from the drug and she couldn't for the life of her think of a way out of this mess. She ate and drank the wine knowing it was not exactly great for the baby growing inside her, but also knowing it was a whole lot better than the alternative. If she angered him in any way, who knew what the repercussions would be?

Although the food was deliciously prepared, the taste barely registered. It was some kind of meat casseroled with wine and herbs with a sweet potato mash and steamed green beans. It was presented beautifully, as if by a trained chef.

Think, think! She thought to herself.

There has to be a way to escape! Maybe pretending to go to the bathroom and climbing out the window? But she was sure he was a lot cleverer than that. *God, please let someone help me!* She lost composure for a second and swayed a bit. He jumped up.

"Are you okay?"

"Just a little woozy," she replied, gaining composure very quickly and smiling sweetly at him.

It worked and he smiled, sitting back down again.

"This meal is delicious," she said. "No one has ever done anything like this for me before."

He looked into her eyes intently with that cold, icy stare.

"I knew you'd be different and would appreciate my efforts," he smiled that robotic smile of his, looking almost amused.

"Wait till you see dessert!"

Dessert consisted of a decadent chocolate cake, dripping with melted chocolate and whipped cream. It really was to die for! Not literally, she was hoping.

He was a very good cook and the house was spotless. He would make some woman a good husband one day, if it wasn't for the fact he was completely and utterly unhinged! Such a shame, all the gorgeous ones are either mental or totally imaginary. She felt a twinge of despair but was careful not to let it show on her face.

She wondered what would happen once the meal was finished. She felt a little as if she was on death row, having one last sensational meal before being sent to the death chamber. There was no doubt that what he had in mind would be anything but normal and possibly end with her murder. Sex, she was sure he wanted that, as she remembered his hands all over her on the couch while she was semi-conscious. But what else was in store? Just what kind of deviant was he to kidnap and drug his dates? Why bother with the special treatment if he was just going to rape and murder her? Or was there some other reason behind the meal, etc? Was it like some sort of ritual? What if she did something wrong and displeased him? She really didn't want to find out the answer to that question. He looked extremely strong and she knew he could overpower her easily. She would just play along and try not to die straight away, if that was possible. She had no idea what his next move would be.

"I'll go and draw you a bath, my love, before we retire," he said smiling that strange, unemotional smile again. "You just relax and I'll be back in a jiffy."

She smiled back at him, panicking inside. *Bath. Retire. God, how was she going to get out of this?* And if she played along and actually had sex with him, would he spare her life? Would she wind up dead afterwards? For now, bending to his will was the only plan she had to save her life. She would do as he wanted and try not to show fear. She didn't want him to snap, although she was quite sure he'd snapped a long time ago!

He was back in a few minutes and lifted her up in his arms, effortlessly carrying her to the bathroom. The bath was filled with rose petals and the scent of lavender. It seemed as though hundreds of scented candles burned everywhere. He very gently put her down onto a chair and started to unbutton her dress. She tried not to flinch or act scared in any way, but could hear her heart beating. It was so loud in her ears she was worried he could hear it too. But he was much too focused on the task at hand. He very carefully undid each button and then softly slipped the straps of her dress over her shoulders. They fell down, resting on her hips. His eyes were glued to her breasts and his hands trembled slightly. He reached behind her and expertly undid her bra and slowly pulled it forward and then pulled the straps down each arm. As his gaze fixed on her naked breasts she was more than a little terrified of what he would do next.

"So beautiful, as I always knew they'd be," he sighed and looked up at her face.

She looked into his eyes and tried to smile, feeling very self-conscious and literally stripped bare. He lifted her to her feet and her dress fell to the ground. Luckily she wasn't really showing and he didn't notice that her stomach was slightly rounded. She was certain the pregnancy would have angered him. He slipped his thumbs inside her panties and gently pulled them down and then sat her down again as he pulled them over her feet.

He stood there for what seemed like an eternity transfixed on her nakedness. She shivered and he noticed it.

"Oh, I'm sorry! Of course you must be getting cold." He bent down and scooped her up into his arms again and lowered her down into the bath. "You have a nice soak there while I go and get everything ready."

He bent down and kissed her on the forehead and then walked out, closing the door behind him. *Get everything ready? Get what ready? What has he got planned for me?* She placed her hands over her stomach as if protecting her unborn child. Maybe your father will save us if he really is the Ghost. God, I hope someone can save us!

He unlocked the bedroom and walked in. It was exactly as he had left it earlier today and he really didn't need to do anything to get it ready for her. The bed was beautiful, cast iron head and tail boards each fitted with shackles to constrain his guests. The bedding was immaculate. Clean and wrinkle free and of course the sheets were tucked in using hospital corners. The quilt was eider down with an intricately crocheted white cover. His tool box was on the bedside table, open and ready to use. The picture of his dead mother and stepfather sat proudly in a frame next to it. All around the walls were his trophy pictures of his previous "relationships." He hoped Cassandra would not be jealous. She had no reason to be, as he was positive that after tonight she would be his goddess and all those other faceless pictures would mean nothing to him. His excitement was growing again and he knew the time was right to go and get her out of the bath. He was ready for bed. He closed the toolbox, not wanting to spoil the surprise then hurried to the bathroom.

Chapter 18
Into the Lion's Den

The door to the bathroom opened and in he came, looking just like the cat that swallowed the canary. He bent down and pulled the plug out of the bath to let the water drain, then helped her out and started to dry her. Her head was spinning. What was next? There seemed to be no visible way out of this. Every window she'd seen had bars on the outside and all the doors deadlocked without the keys left in. No one escaped him. He made bloody sure of that. He wrapped the towel around her and led her out into the hall and down to his bedroom.

All the time her head was screaming *Run! Run!* But run where? There was no way out and he would catch her easily . . . and then his mood would change. At the moment he was kind and attentive and she didn't want to anger him. She had the baby to think about. If possible, she wanted them both to survive this. They stopped outside his bedroom. He looked down at her and smiled.

"Ready?" he said.

"*Ready for what*?" Her head screamed but she nodded her head and tried not to look too terrified.

He opened the door.

At first she thought it looked okay. The bed looked lovely and room was very clean. But as she looked closer at the bed she saw the shackles and the tool box sitting on the bedside cabinet. It was closed and she dreaded to think what was in it. She looked around and saw pictures on the walls. She pulled away from him to go and look at them, stalling a little and showing interest in his hobby. Maybe he was a photographer and was going to take naked photos of her or something? She looked at first photo and had to stifle a gasp. God, it was horrific! Some poor woman, who was quite obviously dead, was posed in a seemingly provocative position, totally naked. She had bruises all over her grey skin, as well as welts, cuts and scars. Her dead eyes still showed the terror she must have been feeling when she died.

Cassie was trying very hard not to cry, but the horror of what she saw was taking over her body. She moved to the next picture and this one was worse! This woman had clearly been dead for a while before he had staged her for the photo. She was starting to decay and her eyes bulged out of her sockets. Her teeth looked hideously locked in a grimace. Her body was also covered in various welts and scars.

"What killed these women?" She wondered, shivering and thinking that her turn was next.

He was watching her closely and noticed the shiver. He rushed to her side.

"Cassandra, why are you shivering?"

He looked concerned, as if he didn't notice the macabre scene before him. She hadn't gone hysterical like the others, screaming and trying to get away. Begging for their lives like little children. No, she was different as he knew she'd be.

"There are just so many . . . " she said looking around the walls and back at him.

"Please don't be angry, my love. You have nothing to be jealous of. They meant nothing to me. Merely building blocks until I perfected my craft and found that one person who understood me. I knew it was you as soon as I saw you, but you had a boyfriend. I had to be patient until you could give yourself to me completely. They were really just amusement for me while I waited for you."

She forced a smile and then saw the frame on the dresser. She walked over to it and picked it up, almost dropping it when she saw the picture inside it. It was of two older people, a man and a woman, dead with their eyeless sockets staring out and their toothless mouths grinning. She knew one was a woman, as they were naked. Although the man's genitals were missing, he was quite obviously male and the woman's sagging breasts were a giveaway. She turned to him.

"Are these your parents?" She asked, actually wanting to know the answer.

"My mother and the bastard she married," he replied.

He looked almost sad but was intrigued with her. She so far hadn't shied away at all. Things were certainly looking up! He walked closer and took the frame out of her hands carefully setting it back down on the dresser. Then he removed her towel and let it fall to the ground. He took in her nakedness and his lower region started to stir. *Yes, this one will satisfy me,* he thought to himself. *Finally, tonight my feelings will be reciprocated.* He lifted her chin and kissed her very gently on the lips. She returned his kiss which made him almost lose control. He kissed her harder, more urgently now, feeling himself getting harder and harder. God, she wanted him as much as he wanted her. He could hardly believe it!

Cassie was doing her best to stay alive and keep her baby alive. She tried to act as if she enjoyed his advances, though inside she was cringing and crying out for someone to please help her before this lunatic killed her and added her photo to his trophy wall!

Chapter 19
Best Laid Plans

Something was wrong. He could sense it. Their bond was so strong and he knew she was in trouble. But how could he go to her like this? She wasn't asleep or unconscious and would see him as he really was. Then there would be no hope of her ever loving him for real. The dilemma was tearing him apart. He needed to go to her, but needed that safety net— that gateway into the subconscious— to protect himself. If he must go as he really was, it would be only because he'd never let anyone hurt her. Not her. She was his everything and he'd protect her with every fibre of his being. She carried his child, and although the child was practically human he worried that Cassie would never be quite sure.

The child . . . of course! Why did he not think of it before? His son was his way in.

Cassie was getting desperate now. The situation was hopeless. How could she escape this man without harming her child and without having to do the unthinkable? If her dream lover was really the Ghost, then he'd come to save her. After all, she was the mother of his child and he said he loved her. But why wasn't he here if that was the case? She was trying to think straight, but the nutter had his tongue down her throat and was touching her everywhere!

She tried to moan and feign pleasure all the while trying to devise a plan to get out of there. When did the Ghost come to save women about to be murdered? Usually when they were unconscious or on the brink of death . . . and maybe that was the key? He visited her in her dreams, so maybe the only way for him to help was through the subconscious mind. It sounded insane, almost as insane as her bedroom companion. But then, everything over the last six months had been wildly insane. Maybe if she could somehow make herself blackout without harming the baby, her dark haired man could save her?

Her captor picked her up in his arms and lowered her onto the bed. She was totally naked and felt on display and totally vulnerable. He started to put her hands and feet into the shackles.

God, it's starting, she realized, starting to panic. *Think Cassie, think!* She screamed inside her head.

He straddled her, naked with his enormous erect penis hovering above her. He was quivering and getting very anxious. Cassie's heart was beating overtime again and she was wondering what he was going to do next.

God how can I make this freak knock me out without killing me and harming my baby?

He leaned over toward the dresser, reaching for the toolbox. As he opened it with one hand, Cassie was sure he'd see the horror she found impossible to hide! His toolbox . . . God, it was exactly like an interrogator's or torturer's stash, filled with knives, a hacksaw, a power drill, various ropes, a Taser, a couple of gas lighters, pliers, secateurs, and a tool that looked like a leather punch. Okay, so now she knew what caused all those scars on those poor women hanging on his wall. But what was she going to do to avoid ending up as one of them?

Her mind was racing and she knew she'd better think of something soon. What if she could get him to choke her? Not too much so as to kill her, but enough to make her semi-conscious and give "Him" a gateway in. It was a risk. The nutter might go too far and kill her. But it was the only plan she had and dying by choking suddenly seemed a welcome idea considering the alternative!

He was deciding which tool to use first. He picked up the drill and then put it back down. Then he picked up the lighter and put it back down. He picked up the pliers and held them toward Cassie, as if asking for her input. She tried to act as calm as possible. She needed this plan to work. She shrugged and shook her head at the pliers, and he smiled and picked up the Taser. She faked a laugh and shook her head again. He picked up the rope. She pursed her lips as if in deep thought.

"Do you have something a little more feminine, like a silk scarf or stocking?" she asked, smiling.

He got very excited and jumped up, running to his dresser and pulling out a lovely cashmere scarf.

He ran back to Cassie holding up his prize and looking very pleased with himself.

"Oh yes, I think I'd like that one very much," she said, convincingly. "That's just what I like to start foreplay with."

He jumped back on the bed and quickly wrapped the scarf around her neck. He looked like a little boy all excited at opening his Christmas present! He straddled her once again and if his face wasn't enough to show his utter excitement, then the size of his huge organ, which seemed to have grown yet another inch, definitely was!

"Okay, now remember, Sweetie, not too hard as to kill me but hard enough to almost make me pass out," cooed Cassie. "That's how I like it, just about to the brink of death. If you go too far you'll miss out on playing with all those other lovely toys and me showing how I can help relieve this swelling," she said demurely, looking at his penis. "We wouldn't want that now, would we?"

He shook his head like a little boy, giggling and carefully tugging at the scarf around her neck.

Cassie tried to relax, but suddenly saw another face in front of her, an ugly contorted face with veins popping out. It screamed at her, *You fucking little bitch, say no to daddy now, will you? I'll kill you, you fucking little whore. Just like your bitch of a mother. You deserve each other and after I kill you I'll go after her.*

She started to panic and didn't know what was happening! The scarf wasn't even very tight yet. The ugly man disappeared and her captor looked puzzled at her expression, then annoyed. He began wrapping the scarf around each hand preparing to give her a good choking.

Then Cassie saw another face standing at the foot of the bed, a beautiful and reassuring face. He was smiling and had his finger to his lips as if to tell her to not give him away. But how was he here? She was still fully conscious, the choking hadn't started properly yet. How was it possible that her dark haired man had materialized? She knew his conduit was an unconscious mind.

What did it matter as long as he came to save her? She smiled back at him, relieved and grateful, and waited for him to make his move.

Chapter 20
Unmasked

My hero walked around to the side of the bed. My captor saw him and instinctively grabbed for a knife, diving off the bed. My hero looked down at my attacker's now flaccid penis and smiled, mocking him. This made the nutter absolutely furious and he lunged with the knife, only to be very easily forced to the ground. The knife was instantly removed from his hand.

"Why must you kidnap these poor women and torture them for your own pleasure?" he asked.

"Cassie loves me," he screamed. "I've been nothing but kind and attentive to her. Ask her!" he looked at me expecting me to corroborate his story. His eyes looked into mine trustingly, almost expecting me to run to his rescue.

"No, you're wrong," I said looking at my lover and smiling. "I went along with you to prolong my life, waiting for the man I truly love to come and save me."

If he had a heart I believe it would have shattered then and there. He looked hurt and betrayed. But his mood soon turned to rage and he tried to lunge at me to take his revenge. He didn't get far.

"Tsk, tsk," said my dark haired angel. "You wouldn't hurt a lady now, would you?" He had his arm around the nutter's neck and restrained him effortlessly.

I tried to loosen my shackles and then felt my baby kick.

Thank God, I thought. *You're okay.* I put my hand on my stomach protectively and looked up to smile at my love.

He had a look of horror on his face.

"Cassie, you need to get out of here now. Go now, please!"

She didn't understand and looked to him for answers.

"I can't leave. I am shackled to the bed!"

He was panicking and she didn't understand why. Her dark haired angel looked around as if searching for an escape route, then dragged his captive through the bedroom door. Once in the hall he looked sadly at Cassie, closing the door behind him.

Cassie was bewildered and had no idea what had just happened. She was no longer in danger. He'd come to save her . . . why would he want to get away from her?

She heard a man screaming and begging for his life. She almost jumped out of her skin, it was so sudden.

"What the hell was going on?" she exclaimed out loud.

Then Cassie heard a low rumbling sound. At first she couldn't make out what it was, but then realised the noise was . . . *growling!* She remembered the stories of the Ghost ripping assailants to pieces, always accompanied by growling. She wondered how he could possibly do that— morph into a monster and suck the life blood out of criminals. How could her sweet and gentle lover possibly be the same monster that tore these men limb from limb? She needed to get out of these shackles! She wriggled her left hand and tried to get it out of her restraint, but it was too hard only using one hand.

Damn it! She was stuck there until someone decided to free her.

She could hear banging and crashing and snarling and hissing and screaming. It was driving her crazy. What the hell was happening outside that door?

Suddenly, the door crashed off its hinges and a bloodied body came flying into the room. It was followed by a man. Well at least she thought he sort of looked like a man. He was covered in blood and dived onto the body lunging at its throat. Her former captor writhed on the floor, screaming out in agony. Cassie could hear the creature slurping and sucking.

"Oh God," she thought, "It's drinking his blood!"

She heard a blood curdling scream and then realised it was coming from her. The creature jerked its head up and looked towards her. It had long straggly hair and ice blue eyes, very pale skin and fangs. Blood was dripping from them and running down its chin. The features looked familiar and she realised it was him! Him, the man who had made love to her in her dreams, the man who was the father of her baby. Only he wasn't a man. Instead he was some sort of animal sucking blood out of the body lying on the floor.

She screamed again and frantically struggled to free herself, knowing that it was hopeless. The creature tilted his head sideways and looked at her as if with recognition. He forgot his meal and stood up and started to walk towards her. Cassie screamed and tried again to struggle free but couldn't get out of her shackles.

"No, please don't kill me!" she screamed. "You said you loved me, remember?"

It stopped and looked at her as if unsure of what she was saying. It tilted its head back opened its mouth and let out a piercing shriek.

Cassie fainted.

Chapter 21
Skeletons in the Closet

"Come on Cassie, push!" Hayley said. "He's almost here."

"I can't!" I cried. "It's too hard and I'm too exhausted!"

"You can't give up now, it is almost over," Hayley said, sounding almost angry at me.

I gave it just one last big push and then he was out. I sighed and laid back down on the bed, waiting for Hayley to check my baby and then bring him to me. She seemed to be taking ages and I hadn't heard a single sound coming from him yet.

Why wasn't he crying? I asked myself. *Shouldn't he be crying by now?*

I sat up a little and looked over to where Hayley and Maria were standing. They were hovering over him and both were looking deathly pale.

Oh no, I thought. *He's dead!*

"What's wrong? Why isn't he crying?" I asked, almost hysterically.

They both turned and looked at me, but neither spoke.

"Is he dead?" I screamed, starting to cry.

They both shook their heads but looked as if they were in shock.

"I want to see him!" I jumped out of bed and almost fell on the floor. My legs felt a little like jelly, but I steadied myself and walked over to where they were standing. "I want to see him!"

"Cassie, I . . . " Maria stopped in mid-sentence and then shook her head and looked down at the ground.

I almost pushed her out of the way and looked down at my baby lying on the table. I gasped in horror! He was hideous! No wonder they were in no hurry to show him to me! He was covered in coarse black hair and had big pointy teeth and black eyes and a tail! He looked at me and snarled. I backed away and started to scream.

"No, that's not my baby! He said my baby was like me, not him! Take him away, he's not mine!"

Someone was shaking me as if to snap me out of my shock.

"No, leave me alone!" I screamed. "He's not mine there's been some sort of mistake!"

"Cassie, Cassie! It's okay, wake up!" I could hear Maria's voice off in the distance somewhere. "You're having a nightmare."

I sat up and opened my eyes, instinctively putting my hands on my stomach. Still pregnant, thank God, it was only a dream. Or was it a premonition? I shuddered and looked at Maria.

"It was horrible! I was dreaming I had the baby, but it was a horrible monster!"

Maria leaned over and hugged me.

"I'm not surprised you're dreaming about monsters after what you've been through, Hun."

It slowly started to come back to me— the madman who had kidnapped me, his tools of torture, the room with pictures of kidnapped and murdered women. And then . . . the other man. The other man who transformed from a beautiful, caring, lover into something else! But what exactly was he, a Vampire? Vampires weren't real, they were a just myth. Or were they?

Cassie was pretty sure that her dark haired man was a Vampire. His fangs and blood-drinking kind of gave it away!

So, if the man she dreamt about and the Ghost were one in the same, then what? What had made him change from being human to this other . . . thing? He hadn't hurt her and had most definitely saved her from being tortured, raped and eventually murdered.

"How did I get here?" she asked Maria.

"It's a mystery, my dear. Once again, an orderly found you on the front steps. You were totally naked but wrapped in a blanket."

So he saved me and brought me to the hospital.

"What about the guy who kidnapped me? Do the police know where he lives or who he is?"

"Well, he didn't survive to tell the tale. The Ghost did him over pretty bad!" She said grinning. "If he hadn't, I certainly would have!"

She told me there had been an anonymous phone call to the cops telling them what had happened and where. When they got there they found Micheal Banks with his throat ripped out, his penis ripped off and stuffed in his mouth and practically no blood in his body. Forensics had searched the area but once again couldn't find any evidence of the Ghost, other than the macabre body lying on the floor and the broken furniture and door. There were obvious signs of a struggle, but no physical evidence.

They did, however, find a lot of trace evidence from different females and after seeing the pictures on the walls and his beloved toolbox, decided to do a thorough search of the house and grounds. Using a portable X-ray machine they found untold bones buried in his back yard. Once they started to dig they found the skeletons of fifteen women. Some were badly decomposed, but others died as recently as a few weeks ago. They used the horrifying pictures, dental records and DNA to identify the victim's bodies so loved ones could be notified. He'd obviously been doing this for quite a while.

Cassie shuddered. God, she could quite easily have been one of those women if not for the Ghost. Now she understood what, in his roundabout way, he'd been trying to tell her. They could never be together in the real world because in the real world he looked like a monster and people would certainly notice! *But how did he come to me as a human when I was fully conscious?* It was baffling, but she needed to know the answers. Maybe he'd visit her again and she could ask him. But would she feel the same about him, or would she be scared of him now? She honestly didn't know.

"I am getting quite tired, Maria. Do you mind if I have a little nap now? I'll try not to freak you out with my screaming this time," I said, smiling.

"Of course you can. Best thing right now for you and the baby."

She hugged me again and then left me, closing the door behind her.

I closed my eyes and started to drift off to sleep, hoping in my heart of hearts that I would soon get a welcome visitor.

Chapter 22
They Walk Among Us

Someone was calling my name and touching my hand. I opened my eyes and saw a pretty young nurse trying to rouse me.

Damn it, he didn't come, I thought.

"These policemen want to have a word with you. Are you are feeling up to it?" she asked, smiling sweetly.

I nodded and pulled myself up, asking her to raise my bed so I could sit upright.

They wanted to know what I remembered about the attack. I told them about a hand going over my mouth and blacking out, then waking up in a stranger's house. I told the officers that he cooked me dinner and ran me a bath before taking me into "the room."

"Do you remember how you got away from him?" the younger policeman asked, frowning.

I didn't want to give them any leads or descriptions on the Ghost. I didn't want them to catch him and then find out he was less than human. What would they do to him? I couldn't bear to think about it.

"No, I'm sorry," I lied. "I only remember being choked with a scarf, and then I woke up here."

He nodded, "Pretty much what all the other witnesses have said."

He actually looked a bit relieved. I doubt very much the police wanted the Ghost off the streets, either.

What would I have told them anyway? That the man they were looking for was a Vampire? They'd think I'd hit my head!

They thanked me very much for my time and left.

I felt miserable. Would he ever come back to me? And what if he came in his real form? Would I still love him? It was so much to take in and I honestly didn't have a clue how I was going to feel. I was initially terrified when I saw him, but maybe that was shock. I certainly was not expecting him to change into a Vampire!

The strange thing was, I loved Vampires! Well, at least I loved the ones I'd seen on TV ever since my early teens. I found them very sensual and intriguing and a big turn on! I grew up watching Christopher Lee and Vincent Price horror movies and my favourite movie was Bram Stoker's Dracula. But then, they were fantasies and never in a million years did I think I'd meet a real live Vampire. Or a real, *not so alive,* Vampire! It was a totally different experience being face to face with one, not knowing whether he was going to literally suck the life out of you.

I'd been scared even though I felt sure he loved me and wouldn't have hurt me. The Vampire side of him, at first, didn't seem to know who I was.

Obviously he must have realised, as he'd freed me from my shackles and taken me to the hospital.

I texted Maria and asked her if she could call in before going home and grab my key. I wanted her to bring my laptop and a few toiletries from my house. I needed to do some more research.

I decided to start by researching Vampires. There was a flood of information on the Internet . . . unfortunately, all conflicting. The one common thread was they all needed blood to survive and had fangs. They had once been human. They'd all been turned.

But everything else was very unclear. Some slept in coffins, some slept in freezers and some even hung upside down in caves or closets. Some could change into bats or other animals. Some burnt up in sunlight and some sparkled. Others got weak or dehydrated. All agreed that decapitation or burning killed a vampire, but staking also killed some vampires while paralysing others. I was more confused than ever but was convinced that my lover was definitely one of these creatures.

I thought I'd do some research on the Ghost and see what the online stories said. There were hundreds. All were of a handsome, dark haired stranger arriving just before death and saving another innocent victim from being raped or murdered. No eye witnesses described what I'd seen, and all were either unconscious or incoherent at the time of their rescue.

I was right. He needed that unconscious mind to get in. So how did he come to me? I really didn't understand. I tried to think back to exactly when the moment it happened, the moment he knew he was going to transform. He'd been fine, almost jubilant, as he belittled my captor. Suddenly his face had changed and he looked terrified. It was right after I felt our baby kick. Could that be it? Had the baby been asleep long enough for him to appear human? Had the baby woken up before he'd been able to free me from the shackles? It would certainly make sense and was the only plausible reason for my handsome dark haired man to appear while I was still awake. It also tied in with the other witness statements of being unconscious and not seeing or hearing anything.

There was a knock on the door. It opened slowly and a head poked round.

"Can I come in?" Jenny asked.

Chapter 23
Kindred Spirits

"Of course you can! How are you, Jenny?"

"I should be asking you that!" Jenny answered, smiling.

She sat down on the side of the bed and grabbed my hand.

"I read about it in the paper but didn't realise it was you until Maria rang me. Tell me everything," she said, looking at me as if waiting for me to speak.

I told her how Hayley had just left my place and I was walking back inside when someone put a cloth soaked in chloroform over my mouth. I told her how I slowly became conscious, but my body was still drugged. I could hear a man cooking and singing. He came over and touched me while I was still paralysed. We ate and drank. He gave me a bath. And then I told her about the bedroom and the horrors I'd seen in there.

"Did you see him?" she asked.

By "Him" I knew she meant the Ghost. I wanted to tell her, but I couldn't. How could I describe to anyone what I'd seen? Besides, I felt as if I should protect my dark haired man at all costs. He'd protected us.

I shook my head.

"I fainted," I said, not totally lying.

She looked disappointed but accepted what I said.

"Thank God he was there, Cassie. I shudder to think what would've happened to you if not for him. We both owe him our lives."

She was right, and I owed him mine twice. This was the second time he'd saved me. I told Jenny how I found out about the close call when I was a teenager, explaining why her story had sounded so familiar to me.

She was amazed and it made her faith in the Ghost even stronger.

"He's a wonderful man. A real Guardian Angel," she said. "I thank God for him every day and wish there was some way I could thank him."

"Me too, Jenny, me too," I agreed.

How desperately I wanted to thank him for saving me, not once, but twice . . . and especially for giving me the one thing I wanted most in the world— a baby to love and call my own. I was forever indebted to him and he had no idea how much I loved or needed him. I don't honestly think I'd realised just how much until this very moment.

"I should go and let you get some sleep," said Jenny as she stood up and squeezed my hand.

"I'm quite tired. Really nice of you to come Jenny."

"Let me know if you find out any more on our mystery man. He really does intrigue me," she said as she opened the door. She looked back at me and smiled, and then she was gone.

You and me both, Jenny. You and me both.

Chapter 24
Changing

"It's over," he sighed, his shoulders drooping. "Now she'll never be able to love me and this stupid curse will burden me for yet another lifetime."

It was true. He had allowed himself to hope as he'd done so many times before. He was the hero rescuing damsels in distress only to be tossed aside once his true colours were revealed— his ugly and monstrous side that mortal women found so hideous. Even his own mother had been terrified of him.

Of course there were females of his kind, but he was not attracted to them as he was to the humans. He still felt humanity inside him, although he knew this was seemingly impossible. Perhaps it was because he had once been a doctor, a healer of mankind. He cared to his core about the plight of people, and perhaps some remnant of humanity clung to the monster he'd become. The only way into the mortal world was through the love of a mortal woman. The curse would then be lifted and he could walk among them as if one of them. But for that to happen, the woman would have to first love him in his monstrous form . . . not that of the man she saw in her dreams.

Vampires had such a bad rap. Not all of them were blood sucking fiends. Well, not the fiend part anyway. They had to suck blood to survive and he'd found what he thought was a fair way of doing it, killing two birds with one stone so to speak. Not only was he getting the blood he needed to survive, but in the process was also ridding the streets of vile, disgusting men. He compared himself to a modern day Robin Hood, saving the weak and defenseless and stamping out the bullies.

Certainly there had been very bad Vampires throughout history, which hadn't helped his cause. The most famous of all was, of course, Vlad the Impaler. He'd impaled thousands of people for all the town to see— not exactly the best way to keep yourself anonymous! But there were worse and less known Vampires, too. Gilles de Rais was a French Nobleman who was even one of Joan of Arc's guards. He was very trusted and respected until he was outed and his shocking reality revealed to all. He gave all Vamps a bad name, as his favourite delight was to torture and murder young boys. He would hang them until almost unconscious and then let them down, cuddling them and kissing them and telling them he never meant to hurt them. He'd then go about raping and decapitating them, sometimes even gutting them and pulling out their intestines and wrapping himself in them.

This was why he had the urge to kill evil men. He did not want to be labeled or put into the same category as the vile Vampires who perpetuated the horrible legends. But of course, it was not only males who caused the negative myths. Countess Elizabeth Bathory had kidnapped and murdered young virtuous girls and bathed in their blood. Of course everyone knows that a Vampire stays looking as young as the day they were turned as long as they keep up their blood intake. She just took it that step further and bathed in it as well!

He was ashamed to come from the same bloodlines as any of these treacherous monsters, but unfortunately they were all tied together one way or another. He'd never turned a human, always careful either to kill them or take just what was needed to survive. He, personally, had never been given the choice and, of course, would never have chosen to be like this. He missed feeling the sunlight on his face and the taste of food. He could eat food, but it was tasteless now and served no purpose. He missed interacting with humans most of all. He had been a very social person with a busy medical practice. He missed those days when he'd spend almost every waking hour either at the hospital or partying with friends. He didn't even see his fate coming.

He'd been a little drunk and had stopped for a pee on the walk home. He never saw what or who hit him but remembered coming to in excruciating pain. A young vampire sat beside him apologising for what she'd done. She couldn't have been more than 17 and looked more like a waif than a Vampire. Her clothes were tattered and her face sunken in. She really appeared to be in a bad condition and he found out later he was the first meal she'd had in weeks. She tried to explain to him what she'd done, but he could not comprehend it at the time. In his confusion he thought she was some kind of lunatic and that she'd somehow poisoned him.

In inexplicable agony he begged her to tell him what she'd given him so he could figure out how to stop the pain. She kept telling him she'd turned him into a Vampire. He knew such things did not exist and believed she was some sort of mad woman. Eventually the pain eased, but then the intense hunger took over and he knew he needed to find food. He was so hungry and told the girl he needed to find a meal.

"You need blood," she explained, looking awfully guilt ridden.

"I need to get away from you!" he'd shouted, getting sick of her crazy rantings. "I need to find food!"

She looked heartbroken and bowed her head.

"I'm so sorry. I was very hungry and should have stopped before I drained you. But when I realised your heart stopped beating and I'd killed you, I panicked and fed you some of my blood. I never wanted to be like this and certainly never wanted to make anyone else this way."

She was serious! He stood open mouthed, staring at her. She looked away, avoiding his eyes. He reached into his pockets to see if his money was still there. Okay, so this wasn't a mugging and his keys were still there, too.

"I'm going home now. I suggest you do the same."

He turned and started walking in the direction of his apartment. To his amazement she started to follow!

"What are you doing? You can't come with me!"

"But I have to," she insisted. "I changed you and am now responsible for showing you how to survive."

She looked deadly serious but very nervous at the same time.

"Well, I'm letting you off the hook, so go home!" He shouted and started walking faster.

Again she followed but kept her distance. He sighed but was getting hungrier and couldn't be bothered worrying about her anymore. He got to his front door and put the key in the lock, heading straight for the fridge. He was craving something meaty and juicy and knew he had a big rump steak in the fridge.

He put the frying pan on and chucked in the steak. It sizzled and spat but seemed to be taking forever to cook. He flipped the steak, decided it was cooked enough, and pulled it out of the frying pan. Onto a plate it went, and he picked it up with his hands and took a bite out of it. Cardboard. It was tasteless! He tried another bite from the middle this time. The blood ran down his chin and tasted amazing. The steak itself was bland, like chewing paper. He licked some blood up off the plate. It was delicious and intoxicating. He started to suck the blood out of the steak, it tasted so good. He was like a madman sucking and licking blood and then suddenly stopped, realising what he was doing.

He dropped the steak on the floor and looked at his hands. They were covered in blood. He wanted to lick them but was so shocked at this that he jumped up and ran to the sink. He started to wash his hands vigorously, trying to get the blood off. But no matter how much he washed them he couldn't rid his hands of the smell. *Blood*. What the hell was going on? He went to the fridge and grabbed out an apple. He took a bite— tasteless! He threw it on the floor and grabbed a piece of salami. That too was tasteless. The smell of blood was overpowering and his stomach was yearning for more.

The girl, where was the girl? Had she been telling the truth? He ran to the door and opened it to find her sitting on the doorstep. He ran to her and pulled her roughly to her feet. She shied away and cringed before him.

"What have you done to me?" he screamed. "What in God's name did you do?"

He was shaking her and screaming at her. She lifted her head and looked into his eyes.

"Take your hands off me before I break your arms off!" she snarled.

She was no longer a demure little girl. Her eyes were ice blue and her canine teeth had grown in length. She looked very scary and very angry. He dropped his hands to his sides in shock.

"I tried to tell you, I turned you into a Vampire," she said talking through her teeth and not taking her eyes off him.

"Now, if you will shut up and stop whimpering, I'll tell you what you need to do to survive. It's my duty, as I'm the one who changed you. But once I've warned you and told you how to hunt . . . the responsibility stops there and you're on your own!"

He nodded and sat down on the step next to her, docile and attentive. She proceeded to tell him that life as he'd known it was over, as was his career, until he could get a handle on the blood thing and find a mortal woman to love him!

Chapter 25
Questions

There was a knock on the door and Hayley popped her head around.

"Can we come in?" she asked.

"Of course you can!" I said, closing my laptop. I didn't need them to see what I was researching.

She came in with Moyra close behind.

"Hi Moyra!" I exclaimed as she came over and gave me a hug.

"Oh Cassie, I was so scared when they told me what had happened! I'm so glad you and the baby are okay."

She handed me a box of chocolates and I smiled. "I'm okay now, you can stop worrying."

Hayley pulled a chair over to Moyra and then slumped down into one herself.

"Okay, Miss," she said. "Start from the beginning and don't leave anything out!"

It was more like an order than a request, but I didn't mind and started telling them what had happened. The nightmare had started with Hayley leaving my driveway . . .

"He was waiting for you when I left? Oh, I'm so sorry! I didn't notice anything."

"Neither did I Hayls, and it's not your fault."

I smiled at her and continued with my story. Moyra interrupted a few times with some choice words and looks of disgust. Hayley just looked on horrified, so relieved I'd made it out alive.

"Just wish I could have gotten my hands on the bastard!" Moyra said when I finished my tale of horror. "He wouldn't be hurting anyone else after I'd finished with him!"

Both Hayley and I burst out laughing.

"He's dead, Moyra! The Ghost killed him!"

"Oh, that's right, Petal," she said in that lovely English accent. "Did you get a look at him at all?"

I shook my head and looked at the floor.

"No, I didn't see him, but he's certainly a hero and saved me and my baby's lives. I'll forever be grateful to him."

"Of course you will, dear," she said patting my hand. "Better get back to the asylum now and let you two chat, take care love."

"Okay you, spill!" Hayley said when Moyra left.

"What do you mean?" I asked.

"You may be able to fool the cops and Moyra, but you can't fool me. You saw him, didn't you?"

I hadn't mentioned my dark haired man to Hayley yet. I'd spoken of him only to Maria, who didn't yet know I'd seen him transform into a Vampire. I didn't quite know where to start.

"I'm not sure what I saw, Hayls. I'm trying to work it out in my head. When I have the puzzle solved, you'll be the first to know. I promise."

She seemed unconvinced but accepted my explanation. After kissing my cheek she left me to my thoughts. The truth was, I was still questioning my own eyes. How could I have seen what I did? Was it a dream, or was he really a Vampire who somehow came to me in human form, bringing wild, passionate love to my dreams? I didn't have the answers but definitely needed to find some quickly.

I picked up my laptop and typed "Vampire" into the Google search once again. I'd literally spent hours going through all the different so called expert accounts and now was more confused than ever. If he really was a Vampire, that meant he needed blood to survive. Where did he get this blood from, then? Was he skulking around the streets at night, waiting in the dark for a victim to approach? Somehow I just couldn't imagine him to be like that. He was so loving and caring in his human form. But I'd seen him drinking blood from my attacker. Maybe he only drank the blood of bad men after he had stopped them from hurting someone? I'd seen the rage he possessed when he was throwing Michael around. For God's sake, the police had found the nutter literally drained of blood! It kind of started to make sense. My dark haired man was a Vampire, but he was using his strength and power for good, not evil. He only killed horrible criminals and at the same time satisfied his need for blood.

Surely this didn't make him evil? The men he'd been killing for the last twenty years were definitely evil, and he was doing justice to the human race by getting rid of such monsters.

I had to admit that the sight of him in his real form had scared me— scared me a lot. But he hadn't hurt me and instead rescued me and brought me to the same hospital he brought me to before. I had so many questions and knew that only one person could answer them. But was I ready to let him in again? Would he come back after obviously terrifying me? I hoped so, as I really didn't want to think about my life without him.

Chapter 26
Tomorrow Does Come

The weeks went by and more and more stories of women being saved by the Ghost appeared on the news and in the papers. I'd never seen him again, which made me sadder than I could ever imagine. He'd been in my life for 20 years and to just disappear . . . well, it left me feeling like I'd lost a part of myself. I was grieving terribly for that loss. I'd been home from the hospital for a couple of months now and was spending most of my time organising the nursery and looking forward to the birth of my baby. He was a boy, just as his father said. I had no name picked out for him yet and thought how nice it would be to name him after his father . . . if I'd known his father's name that was!

I was still a little uneasy and often wondered if my baby would be born normal, even though all the scans indicated he was fine. I had four weeks to go and my bags were all packed. Maria was my significant other for antenatal classes and the birth, and of course Hayley was my midwife. I was surrounded by people who loved and cared about me, yet still felt so hollow and empty inside. Thank goodness for my baby, who gave me so much to live for and look forward to. Never in my dreams of having a baby, however, did I ever imagine I'd be doing it alone, without the father by my side.

"You promised you'd never leave me," I announced loudly to the room, not knowing whether he'd hear me. "So I'm pretty sure you're still around, watching and protecting me, although you no longer show yourself to me anymore. I know the last time we met I saw you in your true form, and I have to admit it scared me. But I've had a lot of time to think and now realise that's not the real you . . . not really. The real you is the beautiful man who comes to me in my dreams and makes me feel like the most loved woman in the world. The other you is who you are when you are saving innocent people. I love both sides of you, for you could not be one without the other. In whatever form, you care about people. I know that even in your Vampire form you'd never, ever harm me. I totally accept you for who and what you are. Please know this before you decide to stay away forever."

I had no idea whether he had heard me or not, but it was something I needed him to know. Since he never came to me in my dreams anymore, I thought I'd give it one last go.

I went out onto the balcony and thought of the time I'd slipped and fallen. He'd caught me. I was sure it had actually happened now and not been a dream at all. I thought about the first time he had saved me when I was 13, remembering everything now. The first flashback happened when that madman had the scarf around my throat. I'd seen an ugly face appear over the madman's shoulder . .

. the vile countenance of my stepfather. Over the weeks it had all started to slowly come back to me.

I also knew now, without a doubt, that my dark haired man saved me from the car wreck that killed my parents. He'd taken me to the hospital when I was 17. Ever since then, he'd been in my dreams, comforting me and giving me strength and security when I needed it most. *Well, I needed him now . . . so where was he?* I know he heard me because as he said he was always close by, watching and protecting me. I wished with all my heart that soon he'd come back. My life felt so empty without him. He'd tried to warn me that he was some sort of monster, but all I could see was beauty and kindness. Well, now I'd seen the monster, but still loved him more than words could say. Surely that would make a difference?

I turned to walk inside and got a sharp pain in my stomach. Suddenly I felt a terrifying, wet gush between my legs. I thought my waters had broken and went to the toilet to check. How shocking to see it was actually blood! I sat on the toilet, panicking and crying.

Please, let my baby be okay! I pulled my mobile phone out of my bra and rang Hayley.

I was in such a state she could hardly understand me.

"Calm down, Sweetie. Tell me what's going on."

"I'm bleeding, Hayls," was all I managed to get out.

"Shit," I heard her say under her breath. "Don't panic, Cass, call an ambulance and I'll ring the On

Call Surgeon and Maria and meet you at the hospital."

"S-Surgeon?" I stuttered.

"Hang up now and call the ambulance," she shouted at me.

She was gone. I dialled 000 and told the operator what was happening. I went looking for a clean pair of underwear and a pad. Got my handbag and keys and went outside. I sat on the steps, forlorn and anxious, waiting for the ambulance.

I'm scared! I don't won't to lose our baby! Are you there? Can you hear me? I need you now, I sobbed.

The ambulance arrived and the paramedics put me onto a stretcher, asking me loads of questions. I was more miserable than I'd ever been in my life. I felt so lost and was petrified. The thought of losing my baby was more than I could possibly bear.

We arrived at the hospital and Hayley and Maria were waiting in the ambulance bay. The paramedic was saying something about my BP being 160 over 100 and the foetal heart rate being 76. I knew this was not good and was crying and asking Hayley to help me.

"It's going to be okay, Hun," Maria said. "Hayley has gotten hold of the surgeon and they have an OR ready and waiting to get that baby out ASAP."

She was trying to smile, but I could see she was worried. Hayley hooked me up to a machine to check the baby's heartbeat and contractions. I wasn't having any contractions, but the baby's heartbeat was dropping.

Where was he? Good God, couldn't he see our baby might be dying? He said he loved me, so why was he letting me go through this horrible time alone? I felt very angry at him, but at the moment and was so worried about my baby I couldn't think straight.

"We are here, Cass," Hayley said. "It will all be over soon."

Hayley and Maria undressed me and put me into a gown. Then they moved me onto the theatre table. Not exactly how I pictured the birth of my baby . . . but as long as they saved him I didn't care how they did it. The anaesthetist started to put a needle into my hand and I could see the surgeon with his back to me talking to Hayley.

I was praying inside my head.

Please save him. Please save my baby!

They were talking very quietly and I couldn't hear what they were saying, but Hayley looked very worried. The anaesthetist put the mask over my mouth and nose and started to say something about being sleepy. The surgeon and Hayley walked over.

It was him! He was here! He had come to be with me after all. Only he was dressed as a doctor and had a scalpel . . .

I came round to hear my baby crying. Still groggy, I managed to ask if he was normal. I heard Hayley giggle and say he was perfect. Thank goodness. I don't know what I thought, but at least he was not born looking like a monster.

"Is he still here?" I asked Hayley.

"The baby? Of course he is! I'll bring him to you in a minute."

I hadn't meant the baby. I'd meant Him the baby's father . . . the man of my dreams. But of course, as my head cleared I realized Hayley didn't know about my baby's father. She brought my little one to me. He was perfect with gorgeous olive skin and dark hair just like his father's. I smiled as she put him next to me. I'd never been so relieved to see anyone in my life.

"Hello there you, you gave your mummy quite a scare," I said kissing him on the cheek.

"Not to mention your Aunty Hayley!" Hayley added, positively glowing with happiness.

"Is the doctor who delivered him still here?" I asked, trying not to sound too eager.

"Alexi?" Hayley asked surprised. "He was on call and only came in to deliver your baby. He said he'll pop in tomorrow, though."

"Alexi," I said, looking at the baby in my arms. "What a perfect name."

I felt so fulfilled and content. My baby was safe and He was back! Everything was well with the world again. I could hardly wait for tomorrow to come . . .

ABOUT THE AUTHOR

I'm a life-long fan of paranormal romance and *The Man of my Dreams* is the first novel in a series. The sequel (*Be Careful What You Wish For*) is nearly complete and nearing the editing stage. My inspiration for this series lies close to my heart, for I have my own dark haired man of my dreams, Barry. I am also a big fan of the short lived TV show *Moonlight* and its lead, Alex O'loughlin. Watching this show gave me the push I needed to start writing

I am a stay at home mum of 4 children and write whenever I get the chance. Writing is and always has been my passion. My books are for you - my fans, who share my love of romance and everything paranormal. I hope you will continue on this journey with me and come to love these characters as much as I have.

Made in the USA
Charleston, SC
26 October 2013